A Heavenly Christmas

Based on the Hallmark Hall of Fame Movie
Written By Gregg McBride

Rhonda Merwarth

ISBN: 978-1-947892-15-6

www.hallmarkpublishing.com
For more about the movie visit:
http://www.hallmarkchannel.com/a-heavenly-christmas

Table of Contents

Chapter One

Eve Morgan sighed as the Christmas song blaring through her alarm clock pulled her out of a deep sleep. "Wasn't it just Thanksgiving?" she murmured to herself. The days were passing faster than she'd realized. She changed the station to a financial report program and slid out of bed.

Though it was clearly cold out with a thick layer of snow covering the trees and ground outside her apartment complex, Eve was cozy in her silky gray pajamas. She padded her way across her smooth tile floor and started her day. Shower, dress, makeup, hair: all finished right on time. She had her schedule down to a science, and she prided herself on it.

Her brain was already running down the massive list of things she needed to accomplish that day. New client cold calls, stocks review for existing clients, meetings… It would all get done, and she'd stay as late as it took to ensure that.

When she got into her kitchen, she saw her cat perched on the countertop and shook her head. That doggone cat was so stubborn, refusing to stay on the ground where she kept trying to move him, but oh well. She could indulge him. "Good morning, Forbes," she said lightly, putting down her cell phone on the granite counter and shifting to the drawer where she stored the cat's food. "We need to look at your portfolio," she teased the animal. "I think it's time to diversify."

The cat meowed its opinion on the topic. At least her clients showed more enthusiasm for her suggestions. She'd helped them make a lot of money, and they appreciated that—and her.

She slid the bowl across the counter to the cat. "There ya go." With a smile, she grabbed her phone, taking a peek at the stock app she'd pulled up. "Catnip is trading up, ooh!" Eve grabbed a bottle of water from her stainless steel fridge, then added to the cat, "All right, text me if you need me."

Forbes ignored her teasing comments, focusing on his meal.

Eve stepped out her front door, locking it behind her, then headed to the elevator. Before the doors could shut, her neighbor Ruth slipped in, dressed in what could only be described as a garish green Christmas sweater. Her Yorkie was curled up in her arm, as cozy as a bug. The dog was rather yippy and not that friendly to anyone but Ruth.

"Hello, Eve," Ruth said with a smile as she moved

to the back of the elevator. Her dark skin was glowing with her happy mood, and she hummed under her breath—probably a Christmas song. The woman had been singing them since early November.

"Hey, Ruth." She could see the red and green lights on the sweater blinking in the elevator door reflection. "Wow, that is some sweater," she said as tactfully as possible.

"Well, thanks!" She could hear the perkiness in Ruth's voice. Her neighbor loved the holidays and was always inviting Eve to participate in this or that Christmas celebration in her apartment next door. Eve always declined, not really one for parties—or holidays, to be truthful. Thankfully, the walls were thick enough that she barely heard the ruckus. "I could pick you up one. There are quite a few left."

Oh, heavens no, Eve thought with a mental shudder. Totally not her style. She replied to a client's text, confirming their upcoming meeting time later today. "That's okay," she said to Ruth in what she hoped was a non-horrified tone. "I think that is a one-sweater-per-building sweater."

She stepped out onto the sidewalk and made her way to her office, scrolling through her phone at her emails. Her heels clacked solidly on the concrete. The morning air was crisp. It felt like winter even though it was technically still a few days away. Christmas decorations covered all of downtown Chicago in preparation for the holiday festivities. People were bundled up in their warmest gear as she strolled past them, barely glancing up from her phone.

Her brain was already whirring with the day's tasks and the potential clients she wanted to reach out to. One in particular would be a sweet success to acquire. She dug up his office number and dialed him, mentally prepping herself and getting into saleswoman mode.

But it didn't matter. The client was already on vacation for the holidays, diving in the Caymans. Fighting back her surprise and disappointment, she left a message asking him to call her back when he returned to work.

A Santa ringing a bell caught her attention for a moment, and she grabbed a few bucks from her pocket, dropping them into the Santa's cup. There, her good deed for the day. She dialed the next call in line.

As she entered her building and walked back to her office, she continued chatting on the phone with her current client, briefly noting that the office was decorated for the holidays, too. Bright lights were strung across cubicles, along with sparkling garland and wreaths filling every visible surface. Well, not in *her* office—she didn't have time for such things. Her apartment wasn't decorated, either.

Why bother when you were just going to take it down a couple of weeks later? It seemed like a waste of time.

Eve ended the call, tucked her phone into her pocket, and went to the coffee station, greeting her coworker Carter as he prepared a fresh, steaming cup of java for himself. The thick smell filled her nose, and she could almost taste the concoction.

"Coming to the party tomorrow?" he asked, pouring a dollop of creamer into his holiday mug.

She chose a plain one for herself and grabbed the coffee decanter. "What party?"

He looked over at her in disbelief. "The… office Christmas party."

"Oh. Right." Yet again, she realized how fast December was flying by—and how much work she still had to get done before the end of the year to meet her personal goals. These Christmas events took up important business hours when she could be doing more for the company. Who had time for those kinds of distractions? She poured her coffee mug to almost full.

"Tell me you're not working," he said.

This was their typical conversation every holiday season—okay, not just Christmas time. The company liked to throw parties for everything, and she never went to any of them. "Well, while you're drinking eggnog, I'm going to be improving our bottom line," she tossed over her shoulder as she headed toward her office, clutching her mug.

"I remember being like you once," he said lightly.

"Mm-hmm," she said with a smile. Carter teased her, but he knew her dedication was to Crestlane Financial, to getting things done and making the company prosper. And she was a success at that.

The morning passed in a fury of calls. As a financial consultant, Eve excelled at her job. She kept detailed notes of personal information about her existing clients, and potential clients, to make them feel important. Small things like that could make a difference. She kicked up her heels on her desk and rang up a potential client she'd been wooing, chatting with him for a few minutes. She asked about his daughter and her dressage lessons.

"Yes, of course I remember," she said, chuckling at his disbelief over her recalling something so minute. Okay, enough chitchat. Time to get down to brass tacks and make this happen. She plopped her feet down on the ground and straightened her spine. "Look, I am just gonna say it and let the chips fall where they may." A hooky line she'd perfected over the years that worked wonders on clients she was pursuing. "Apex East is a solid firm. But what are they doing for you, three percent?" She paused then dropped her bombshell. "I can double it."

There was a moment of silence, then he said in his rumbling voice, "Okay, I'm interested in hearing your spiel. Let's get together soon."

A warmth filled her chest. She had him! "Drinks tonight?" she said with a smile, then her grin got bigger when he agreed. "Yes, of course, *très bien*! I'll have my assistant set it up."

"Fantastic," he replied.

"Okay. Bye!" She couldn't hold back her giddiness now. This was going to be a good catch for them. Fontaine Fowler was a reputable pharmaceuticals company, and taking them from Apex East would be a solid victory.

Her assistant, Liz, came through the glass door

and paused. "You bought a tree?" she asked in shock, staring with large brown eyes at the scrawny, plastic green tree sitting against Eve's far wall.

"A client gift," Eve corrected.

"What color is that?" she asked, wrinkling her nose.

"Celery?" Anyway, enough of that nonsense. Eve couldn't keep the pride out of her voice as she said, "We need to set up and print a new client signature pack because I'm going to sign Fontaine Fowler."

"That's fantastic!" her assistant declared, beaming. "I thought they were with Apex East?"

"Yeah, but not for long," she said in a singsong voice, getting out of her chair.

Liz clutched a pack of folders to her chest. "That's why you're my idol."

She knew the woman admired her, but hearing words of affirmation along that vein gave her a flush of pleasure. Eve had fought hard to get where she was, and it made her feel good to have her successes recognized by those around her.

"I'm going to sign one new client before the new year, and I'm going to beat out Carter for that partnership." This was finally hers, the goal she'd worked long hours day after day for. Victory was on the horizon, and her dreams were about to come true.

Not that she would be content to sit back and rest. No, after she became partner, she had big ideas to help the company be even more aggressive in finding new clients and maintaining their existing ones. Eve lived and breathed her job.

Leaning over to check something on her computer, she instructed her assistant to book a table for the City Club at six and to note that she had a conference call at twelve-thirty with Gibson so she'd get him on the line.

"Conflict," the assistant said plainly. "You have lunch with your brother today."

Eve closed her eyes and groaned. *Crud.* "That's today?" Apparently, the refrain for the day was going to be about how fast time was flying and how she couldn't squeeze in non-work distractions—not when there was so much to do before the end of the year. Every second counted. The pressure of looming deadlines made her chest tighten.

Seeming to predict her next thought, Liz added, "And you told me to not let you cancel again since you have three times already."

Eve shook her head, scrambling to figure out a plan to squeeze it in and still make her meeting. "You know what? We'll book the conference room for noon. That way, I can have half an hour and catch up with him."

"Okay," Liz said briskly.

"Thank you!" she hollered as her assistant left.

A half hour would suffice. Her brother would understand. This really was a crazy time of year for them. He knew how it went—she'd explained it to him enough, anyway. Eve pushed the thoughts from her mind and focused on the rest of her morning tasks. Emails had to be answered, and they'd wait for no one.

"Hey!" Eve said cheerily as she walked into the glass-walled conference room. Her brother, Tyler, and his two sons were there waiting on her. "I didn't know you were bringing the boys!" She waved them toward her and gave them big hugs. "What a great surprise!"

"We wanted to make sure you're real," Caleb, the oldest boy, said.

Her brother laughed at the flippant comment.

"Where were you hiding?" Bobby, the younger, asked, peering up at her.

"Hey," Tyler said in a sterner tone, clenching the boy's shoulders. "Manners."

All right, the comments from the boys stung her a bit; her smile wavered. She fought off the flare of negative emotion and said lightly, in an effort to change the subject, "Hmm. Okay, so big question. What do you want for Christmas?"

"You already gave us something," Bobby said.

"What?" She frowned. She hadn't done any holiday shopping yet; she never had the time.

Not that *she* did it—Liz helped out with those things. But she liked to give Liz the ideas for gifts, and that had to count for something.

"A company fruit basket." Bobby's voice was flat.

She winced. Big, big fail. She loved her nephews and couldn't believe she'd done something so bone-headed. How had that happened? Lines must have gotten crossed somehow. She'd have to pull Liz aside and see where things went wrong. "Oh. Okay, so uh, what do you think about... bikes?"

The boys gasped and yelled in unison, "Bikes? That's awesome!"

At their pleased expressions, some of her guilt faded. She'd make it up to them. This year's present would blow it out of the water.

"That's... that's too much," her brother protested.

"No, it's fine!" she said, patting his arm to try to convince him. The more she thought about it, the better the idea seemed. Bikes were the perfect gifts for the boys—they loved being outside whenever the weather was good. At least, that was what her brother had told her, anyway. "It's for Christmas. It only comes once a year. Thank goodness," she added under her breath. "Come on," she said to her nephews, guiding them toward the table. "Look what I got for you. Let's have some cookies. Yum-yum."

As she poured them drinks, she apologized to Tyler about the change in lunch plans, explaining she had a conference call she couldn't move.

"Please tell me you're still coming for Christmas," Tyler said instead, not addressing her apology.

Eve froze for a moment.

"Sherry's making your favorite. It's the, uh, special green beans," he continued.

Eve grimaced and purposely didn't look at her brother. That familiar guilt came back, hot and heavy and sitting in a lump in her stomach. Every year, he nagged her about coming to the house, and she often did. Why, she was just there last... no wait, was it two years ago? Maybe three? Anyway, it was pretty recently.

Her brother thrust his hands into his pockets, disbelief ringing in his voice as he scoffed. He always could read her. "It's Oak Park. It's a half-hour cab ride."

She finally turned to him, shaking her head with regret. She had to make him understand. "But I'm just so busy."

Tyler sighed. "Eve…"

"I'm about to make partner," she emphasized as she poured herself some coffee. The boys were chatting at the table about what cookies they wanted to try. "I mean, I'm this close. You know, Chris Lane hasn't even nominated someone for partner in ten years." She was going to be the one nominated. Then Tyler would support her in this.

Tyler sipped his own coffee and gave her a cursory glance. "That's great, sis." His voice was chilly.

She hated letting him down, having their old, familiar argument crop back up again. The one where he called her a workaholic and she protested that she wasn't, that she was just as passionate about her work as he was about his family. "But?"

He sighed again. "Look. I know we didn't have a lot when we were kids, but we had each other."

She rolled her eyes. *Here it comes.* So predictable. Tyler didn't understand her drive, never had. And to bring their past into it? Okay, yeah, their family had always been tight on money. So?

"Now you're working all the time," he continued. "I mean, what about the rest of your life?" He waved in the direction of her nephews, the gesture saying more than words could.

She didn't have a family of her own. Not like he did.

"I'll get to it," she protested. And she would. On *her* schedule, not because people were pressuring her. She wasn't like Tyler, who lived for his kids and wife and didn't have bigger aspirations for himself. She wanted more. At least, for right now. There would be time later for all of that stuff—the house and kids and white picket fence.

"When?" His voice warmed up with the strength of his convictions. "You never see your family. You put all your relationships on the back burner."

"No, that's not true," she lobbed back. Irritation at his words festered in her. And she did see her family, when she could. Truth be told, maybe it wasn't as much as they wanted her to, but she made the effort.

"Really? When was the last time you let anyone in?" Tyler took a sip of his coffee.

Ugh, and here we go, she thought with a wry smile. Moving on to the fact that she didn't have a significant other. The argument pattern was as familiar as it was tiring.

"Well… actually, I have a relationship," she declared, putting her mug on the table. Time to end this argument. She wanted to enjoy their remaining minutes together, not bicker. "My relationship is a long-distance relationship, because… my boyfriend is in the future." She slugged his upper arm, and he groaned, but a peek of a smile warmed his face.

Tension leaked from her shoulders, and she relaxed. Crisis averted. She knew the topic wasn't dropped, and he'd be back to poking at her about it soon enough. But for now, she could just enjoy their company.

"Eve," Liz said, entering the room. "Can I talk to you for a second?"

"Yes," she said, spinning to face her assistant. "Definitely. But first, go get my nephews some bikes."

Liz just eyed her, and Tyler gave a heavy sigh.

"Eve," he started, but she waved Liz away to go on her errand.

"They're going to love them," Eve assured her brother when the woman left. See? She could do this— have family time *and* do some personal shopping. She'd picked out the gift idea on her own. What did it matter who bought it?

Wasn't he always telling her it was the thought that counted?

The rest of the day flew by in a flurry of meetings, and before Eve knew it, it was time to meet the doctor for drinks. She shut down her computer and exited her office. The whole building was dark. When had everyone left? She'd been too busy to notice.

"Taxi!" Eve hollered with a frantic wave as she stepped out of the building into the bitter-cold night, striding across the snow-sloshed sidewalk toward the street. One cab slowed down, so she rushed across the asphalt to catch it.

Only to have a man reach for the door handle at the same time.

"Oh, sorry," she said to him on reflex, pulling back.

"Sorry," he echoed and did the same.

Taking his apology as affirmation that the cab was hers, she reached for the handle again—at the same time he did.

She eyed him. Snow coated his thick black hair and dotted his eyelashes. He was striking with a strong jaw and piercing, dark eyes. Still, she didn't have time for this. "I was here first."

"Well, I'm pretty sure we were here at the same time," he answered smoothly. His voice was warm and rumbling. After a moment, he said, "Uh, are you going north?"

She nodded. "Yeah, north side."

He smiled, and the gesture made her stomach flip for some odd reason. "Me, too. Wanna share?"

She glanced down for a moment, pondering it, then shrugged. "Okay." Why not? She could be magnanimous. So long as she made her meeting on time.

They got in and rode down the street, him tucking a guitar case between his legs, resting the bottom on the floor. She flipped through her email notifications on her phone and made brief, idle chitchat with the stranger. But the Christmas music playing was irritating and distracting. She asked the driver to change the station.

"You don't like Christmas music?" the guy beside her said.

She snorted. "Oh, it goes on and on and on." And every Christmas season, all the stations were inundated with it. Nonstop. How was no one else but her burned out on hearing it so much? *Ugh.*

He started to sing a Christmas song, and she side-eyed him. He stopped.

"Partridges in trees," she said, leaning toward him and waving a hand. "What do those words even mean?"

"I'm pretty sure they're called 'lyrics,'" he said evenly. Funny guy.

"But… they're non-migratory birds. If they did make a nest, it wouldn't even be in a pear tree." The stranger didn't say anything, just stared at her. Whatever. She knew she had a rational point.

When she realized they were close to Madison, she directed the taxi driver to turn onto it.

Funny Guy quickly protested that they should stay on this road because of traffic.

"Yeah, but my stop is first," she retorted.

He tightened his arms around his chest, eyeing her. "Well, you're going to make me late."

"You're going to make me late for a *very* important meeting." She tried to maintain her patience even though frustration was welling in her at his presumption. First, he'd tried to take her cab, and now he was going to possibly ruin her drinks with her prospective client.

No way. So much was riding on this.

"Life-or-death important?" he asked her, brows raised, clearly not believing it was.

"Actually, yes." Her words were firm. She knew this was more important than whatever he was doing. Some kind of open-mic night thing? It could wait.

"Okay," he murmured, giving in.

Thank heavens. She returned her attention back to the driver and instructed him to turn right.

Into a thick batch of traffic.

"Aaaand jingle all the way," her ride partner said flatly.

She sighed. No way could she wait in this traffic. She'd never make it in time. "Well, I'm going to walk." She grabbed a handful of cash and handed it to the driver. "Here. Thank you. Um, good luck with your... guitar thing," she said to the passenger.

"Happy holidays," he told her with a slight wave of one hand.

When the woman exited the cab, Max Wingford told the driver, "Um, you can turn the music back on."

What an odd encounter. Yes, it had left him a touch bristly over being left in terrible traffic... but he was also curious about who the mysterious woman was. Who argued logistics about Christmas songs? Strange, cab-commanding women, he supposed. Ah, well. Time to focus and get his head in the game. His audition needed all of his attention. And he knew Lauren would be grilling him about it tomorrow when she returned from her sleepover at her grandparents'. He didn't want to let her down.

Max finally arrived at the auditorium and stared at the marquee declaring auditions tonight for the Christmas Eve concert being held there. No one seemed to be entering or exiting the building, but he was pretty sure that, even though he was late, he could probably slip in. His guitar case, as heavy as a rock, rested against his back, his hands shaking as he clenched the strap.

Passersby wandered down the sidewalk in the thickening snow, and he stood there for a moment, willing himself to go in. He could do this. Yeah, it had been a long time, and yeah, he was solo now. And okay, he was pretty out of practice, and his original songs weren't all that great anymore without his sister's help...

He couldn't do this. Couldn't make himself step inside. His feet felt glued down, his heart frozen behind his ribcage.

His throat was tight as he turned and walked down the sidewalk.

Away from the audition.

It was probably better this way.

Chapter Two

Max chopped the vegetables for the warm stew he was whipping up. The people at his diner loved it, and he only offered it during the Christmas season, which made it a special holiday treat. He took comfort in the rote action, something he'd grown familiar with since opening the diner. This was where he belonged, not on a stage. Not anymore.

As he diced and julienned, he ignored the sensation in his gut, the one that called him a coward for not doing the audition last night. He'd really wanted to… at least, on some level. But push had come to shove, and he hadn't been able to. He was disappointed in himself. His nerves were a clear sign that it wasn't meant to be. Right?

His niece Lauren came back in the kitchen, distracting him from his thoughts. Her long hair swayed as she walked. "Uncle Max!" she said happily.

Afternoon already? Time had gotten away from

him. He shot her a smile. "Hey, kiddo! Did you have a fun sleepover with your grandparents?"

"Yup!" She settled onto a stool and watched him continue dicing up the veggies. Lauren loved observing him cook and even helping in whatever way he'd let her. She had a good sense of taste for a fifth grader. And he welcomed having her in the kitchen, even if part of him felt like this wasn't exactly the best life for her. But he was raising her, and he had to work, so that meant she was stuck with him here.

He scooped the vegetables into the big pot of simmering liquid. "How about school? Did you guys rehearse that play?"

"Forget about me," she said, smiling slyly. "How was your audition?"

Ugh. "I, uh…" He wiped his hands clean. "I didn't actually make it," he murmured in a quiet tone.

"Why?"

"Traffic jam." Easier to blame that than his own fear. And it *was* kind of true—he was really late because of that woman, and there was a possibility he wouldn't have made it in time anyway. Keep rationalizing your cowardice, Max, his conscience chided. "Sorry, kiddo," he said when he saw her look of disappointment. He hated letting her down, but he just wasn't ready. "Next Christmas, okay?" By then, he'd for sure have his A game back. He hoped.

"But that's 372 days away," she said, eyeing him. She could see right through him.

"It'll go fast." He scooped a serving spoon into the

pot and brought it to her, laden with golden broth. "I'm working on our famous Yuletide Stew," he said as she sipped.

She thought for a moment. "Needs more turmeric."

He frowned. "Turmeric, eh?" He downed the rest of the spoonful to confirm her thoughts, then dug through the spices to find it. The girl was right, as usual.

Lauren gave a small sigh. "Remember when you and Mom used to sing at the holidays and write those funny songs?" The longing in her voice made his chest ache as he had a flash of memory of him and his sister. Sitting around the Christmas tree, him with his ever-present guitar, both of them laughing at their ridiculous lines and getting their whole family in on it.

They'd had such a good time. His sister had been not only his singing partner, but his best friend.

He shook the spice into the stew and said in a low voice, "I remember."

"Why can't you just start again?"

If only things were that simple. Lauren wouldn't understand, though. "It isn't that easy, kiddo."

He glanced over from the pot to see her looking down at the floor, her face unreadable. "'Cause you have me," she said in a hushed tone.

"Of course not," he said, turning his full attention to her. "I *love* having you." He hoped she could hear the truth in his words as he stirred the stew. "I was just never any good without your mom." Since she'd

24

died, everything had changed. He'd lost his mojo. His talent. His inner fire.

"But you *are* good," she protested.

Max saw the meat on the cooking surface was ready to turn. He grabbed the spatula and went to it, flipping it over. "Remember when you told me you were stuck on those lines in your school play?" he asked her.

She nodded.

"I'm stuck, too." The admission was hard to say, but he wanted her to know why he just… couldn't. He put the spatula down and scooped another spoonful of stew for her to sample. "Come on. Turmeric, or not turmeric? That is the question."

She took a sip and gave him a knowing look. "You're trying to distract me, aren't you?"

"How did you guess?" he said smoothly at her smile. So much like his sister—her mom—the kid was too smart for her own good.

"Uncle Max?" Lauren asked as Max tucked her into bed later that evening. "I know you're not a morning person, but is it okay if we get up early and go sledding?"

He tucked a teddy bear beside her. "Who says I'm not a morning person?"

"You said musicians were night owls." She said it in a tone far too mature for her age.

Hah. The child remembered everything he ever told her. He shifted on the bed beside her. "Well, that was before you moved in." He gave a heavy, fake sigh. "Now I never sleep at all."

They grinned at each other, and she snuggled the bear against her chest.

"When Grandma and Grandpa leave, are you going to teach me to play guitar?" she asked innocently.

His heart thrummed against his ribcage. He wasn't ready for the conversation he knew they needed to have. Not yet. "Let's talk about it after New Year's," he said with a forced smile. "Okay?" He patted her leg. "Good night, sweetie. Sweet dreams." He shut off her light, closed the door, and walked into the living room. Eyeing the guitars lined up against the corner, he rubbed the back of his neck and exhaled softly.

On the mantel was a picture of him and his sister, her smile piercing, eyes sparkling, him with his guitar beside her. He picked up the photo and looked at the image, the familiar pain of missing her rushing into him. Since her death two years ago, he felt like he'd aged a hundred years. His whole life had changed. He settled down into his chair and got caught up in memories of a time when life was easier and music was in his soul.

Now, his soul was silent, and he felt empty inside. Like a big piece of him was gone. And he suspected he'd never get it back.

The next afternoon, Carter, a Santa hat tilted on his head, came by Eve's office and handed her a mug full of eggnog. Outside her door, she could hear people chatting and festive music playing. The Christmas party had started, and everyone was having a fantastic time from the sounds of it. Good for them. Part of her wished they were a bit quieter so she could focus, but she knew the parties came with the territory. Oh well.

"Thank you," she said to Carter with a chuckle as she took the offering. "Is this poisoned?" she teased. She knew he wouldn't do something like that, that the competition between them was healthy and fair, but it was fun to harass him.

Instead of laughing, his face turned serious. "A little piece of advice from someone who's been doing this longer." He paused and she eyed him. "I know how badly you want this partnership. And you're probably going to get it. But some really good stuff is passing you by."

She stared at him for a moment, unsure what to make of the frank remark. *Wait a minute.* She knew what this was, what he was doing. "Are you trying to psych me out?" she asked with a smirk.

Carter smiled then and rolled his eyes. "I'll see you tomorrow."

"Oh, don't give up that easily!" she protested.

She could see flashes of emotion pass in his eyes, something that looked suspiciously close to pity. For her. It made her a little uncomfortable. "I'm going home to Christmas carol with my family."

"Okay," she replied quietly. "Have fun."

"You're welcome to join us," he offered.

Right. Because she was so the singing type. "Thank

you. But while you're out caroling, I'm going to be here, signing new clients." He already was aware of this, of course, but she felt she needed to reiterate. This was why he'd admitted that she'd be getting the partnership. They both knew it. Because her work ethic was stronger than anyone else's at the company, and she didn't let anything get in the way of her goals.

Carter gave a brief nod. "Good night, Eve."

"Okay, thanks, Carter!" she said with a wave, then settled down into her chair.

Eve took a sip of the eggnog and grimaced at the thick, creamy liquid. Gross. How did people drink this stuff, anyway? She set it aside on her desk and resumed work.

The reveling outside in the main area continued for hours. But after a while, it was easy enough to shut it out when she kept her attention on the task at hand. She reviewed the stocks banners and scrawled down notes for her existing clients as discussion points on how to improve their portfolio. She had a hunch one tech stock in particular was going to take off—an up-and-coming company with cutting-edge innovation, from what she'd read—and she wanted to be right on the forefront of it when it did.

By the time Eve decided to call it a night the entire building was silent and dark. She closed her office door and walked out. Yes, the work day was technically done, but she could do a little more business on her way back home. No sense wasting the time, right?

She dialed Ted's number and headed out into the

snowy night air, her breath puffing around her in soft clouds. A woman at a food stand called out offering chestnuts, but due to her nut allergy, she declined as she waited on hold.

The woman said "Merry Christmas," but the other side of the line answered, and Eve said into the phone, "Hey, Ted, it's Eve Morgan from Crestlane Financial. I'm just gonna come right out and say it, let the chips fall where they may. I know you're with West Trade Brokers, and I just wanna—"

Eve's high heel slipped on an icy patch, and she hollered in surprise as she flew through the air and fell. Hard.

Her head *thunked* on the sidewalk, and a flash of brilliant pain enveloped her before everything went dark.

Eve blinked her eyes open and looked around in confusion. The room she was in was white, pristine, and she was lying on a bed—a bed that wasn't hers in a room that wasn't anywhere she'd ever been.

What happened? Where was she? Her memories felt scattered, and she couldn't wrap her head around what led her here, to this strange place. She frowned. Why couldn't she remember anything?

"What... ?" she whispered, glancing at the bed— and the white cat lying curled up against her leg in an eerily familiar fashion. Her throat grew tight with emotion as she said, "Snowball?" She reached down to pet his soft fur. Was this real? "Hi, kitty," she whispered. How was he here?

No, this couldn't be possible. Snowball had passed away a long time ago, when she was a kid. She'd loved that cat like crazy.

"You look just like a cat I had when I was little. Except he had a... black tail," she trailed off when she shifted the covers to reveal that this cat, too, bore a black tail.

Something in her chest felt odd. This wasn't right. Nothing felt normal here. Was she awake? Dreaming? In a hospital bed on drugs? She scooped the cat into her arms and sat up on the white bed, looking around again.

What is going on?

"There ya go," she said, letting the cat onto the floor. It scurried under the bed.

Nearby was a mirror; Eve stepped up to it and examined herself. She wasn't wearing her usual dark business outfit. Instead, she had on a silky white dress. *I know I don't own anything like this.* Something was majorly off.

"Miss Morgan," a light voice said from behind her.

Eve spun around to see an older woman with bobbed brown hair, her body also clad in all white like Eve, standing right behind her. The woman's smile was wide and welcoming.

"Hello. I'm Pearl," she said in a smooth tone. "I'm going to be with you during this transition."

Eve stared blankly in shock. "Transition?" What could she be talking about? None of this made sense, and she was starting to feel freaked out, her hands trembling. Everything about this place was weird. Her pulse stuttered in her veins, and she struggled to maintain her usual calm sense of control. She had to be sick or something. That was the only thing that was logical. "Okay. I don't know what kind of hospital this is, or why I'm here, but as you can see, I'm perfectly fine." She looked down at herself, taking stock of her body. "In fact, I've never felt better," she realized. "So, hopefully, you bill insurance—I have 90/10 group coverage."

Pearl chuckled. "We don't take insurance up here."

Eve swallowed. Was she in danger? Why would this woman laugh about that? No matter. She would pay up and get out of here. "Okay, then I'll just, uh, put it on my credit card." She walked over to the white dresser nearby and pulled the top drawer open, searching for her purse.

"Credit cards aren't necessary here, either," Pearl said.

"But... where's my bag?" Eve asked. "Where's my phone?" Panic swelled in her, and she began to dart around the room. Nothing felt right here. Nothing made sense.

"They don't matter here."

Here? Where was *here*? Eve searched the bed to see if maybe her bag was tucked under the sheet. Nothing.

She turned and eyed the woman with suspicion. "Do I have a concussion?"

Pearl chuckled. "No."

Okay, scratch that idea. "But… I am on some kind of medication though, right?" It was the only thing that would explain why she'd have a hallucination like this. The surreal surroundings… Her deceased cat… No personal belongings to help identify her… "'Cause I think I'm having a reaction. Everything… is white."

"Yes," Pearl whispered with a grin. "Isn't it beautiful? So peaceful."

"No, it's not peaceful, it's crazy!" Eve blurted out, frustration pouring into her voice. "Or I am." She eyed Pearl, a sudden suspicion about what was going on coming to mind. "Did Carter put you up to this?" It would be low for him, really low, but maybe he was more desperate for the partnership than he'd let on. Had she underestimated his drive? Had he made her think he was more of a family man than he was?

"No."

"I mean, that is devious," she said, taking hold of the idea. Maybe *that* was what was going on, even if she didn't want to admit it. How well did she really know the man? To plan something insane like this just to get her to back off… "He's got that warm, friendly smile. Wow, he must really want the partnership."

"You know," Pearl said with a knowledgeable shake of her head, "as I see it, he's going to get it."

"Over my dead body," Eve declared hotly.

Pearl made a noise of agreement and pointed at her, brows raised.

Eve frowned. *No. No way.* "What?" The woman couldn't possibly mean…

"Miss Morgan, do you remember when you tripped and fell on the ice and hit your head very hard when you were making that cold call?"

Eve's stomach flipped as a flash of memory swept into her. Oh, right—she was talking to Ted and pitching him when her heel had slipped. But wait… She narrowed her eyes. "How do you even know that?"

Pearl walked toward her and touched her upper arms, nudging her to sit back on the bed. She stood over her and said as plain as day, "Miss Morgan. You are in heaven."

Okay. "Heaven," Eve said, her disbelief certainly ringing through in her voice. *Sure* she was. And cows jumped over the moon—which was made of cheese, of course.

Then she saw the cat she was sure was Snowball walk right *through* a nearby column, coming out on the other side and continuing on its merry way. Right. Through. It.

She gasped and pointed. "Did you see that?"

Pearl sniffed and swiped at her nose casually. "Oh, Snowball does that all the time up here."

"But… Snowball's been gone for a long time." How was she really supposed to wrap her mind around what Pearl was saying, even with the oddity she just saw? Nothing made sense. And yet, something about what she was saying wouldn't stop nagging at her—the way she'd hit her head, and everything had gone black after that.

She bit her lower lip.

Pearl sat down beside Eve and wrapped her arm around her. "Time can be very confusing. But in the meantime, you'll settle in."

"So…" Eve took a deep breath and made herself acknowledge what she couldn't believe—didn't want to believe. "What you're saying is that… I'm… dead."

"But I can't be dead yet!" Eve, clutching the woman's hand, protested as Pearl led her down a hallway past other people clad in white. Her free hand was waving in the air, echoing her disbelief at the current state of affairs. No way. No. Way. "I wasn't even finished living. I never even started… I had all these things to do. I was going to start my own hedge firm and buy a country house and get married—and I never even let myself fall in love." The words flowed hot and furious from her as she poured out her feelings. "It just… can't be over…"

"No, no," Pearl soothed and led her to a nearby bench. "Don't cry, Miss Morgan. We are angels. Angels can't cry."

Eve stared at Pearl in disbelief. "Angels?" How could that possibly be true? Not only was she dead, but she was an angel, to boot? This was all too hard to believe.

The woman patted her on the back, and Eve eyed the hallway, taking everything in in a new light. Were all these people angels? Was she really one now?

"Let's talk somewhere more private," Pearl suggested, gripping Eve's hand. The hall faded away, and just like that, Eve found herself on a serene, isolated beach. The sky was expansive, and soft waves licked the sandy shore. She had on a white wrap, just like Pearl, to protect her from the gentle, cool breeze coming off the water.

No doubt about it. Pearl was telling the truth. No one could vanish and appear at will, not when alive, anyway. Eve was here on this shore, experiencing this place fully. Awake, yes—but not alive.

She was an angel, then.

"So this is it?" she said as she stumbled along the sand beside the woman. "This is the end?" So many things left undone. What was her purpose now?

"Oh, no. We like to think of this as the new beginning," Pearl explained.

"What do we do here?"

Pearl paused in her steps and turned to Eve, leaning back against an outcropping of rocks. "Well, among... other things, we answer prayers. I'm a guardian angel. You've been selected to be a Christmas angel."

Eve blinked. This had to be a joke. "Christmas? Now I know there's been a mistake." She couldn't help the dryness in her tone. After all, she wasn't exactly the world's biggest Christmas fan. Of all the people they could have chosen to be that particular kind of angel, why her? It didn't make sense.

"I agree," Pearl said wryly. "It's not an obvious choice. We have a shortage this season."

"I barely celebrate Christmas," Eve protested.

"Well, now you can."

Right. Eve let out a heavy sigh and looked out at the water. "With all due respect, Pearl, I just don't see myself celebrating anything for a long, long time."

Pearl seemed to choose her words carefully. "Perhaps when you go back, you will change. You're being sent down to answer a Christmas wish."

That got Eve's attention. She swallowed. "I get to go back." She didn't have to stay up here in the all-white weirdness for eternity.

"Mm-hmm. For a week."

Okay, not a lot of time, but she'd make do. "What happens in a week?"

Pearl narrowed her eyes. "Christmas."

"Ohh," she breathed. Duh, of course.

Eve felt Pearl's warm grip in hers, that strange, surreal feeling of everything fading away, and then she was surrounded by a painfully familiar setting. Downtown Chicago, bustling with traffic and pedestrians, Christmas decorations on every stretch of street. The cool air chilled her cheeks, though she was snuggly warm in her black winter coat. She smiled.

"I'm back!" she exclaimed. Hard to believe it, but she'd missed the place. Everything seemed so different now, so alive. The quiet serenity of heaven was a drastic change from the teeming life in the city.

"Mm-hmm," Pearl said, patting her hand and leading her down the sidewalk. "Now, there are rules."

"Rules?"

"Yes, you cannot attract any attention to yourself. No one can know that you are now an angel." They walked past a street vendor, past numerous people milling about on the sidewalk who stopped in their tracks and looked at the two of them.

"Who would believe that anyway?" Eve asked. Except maybe the weirdos who wandered down the street, muttering to themselves while pushing shopping carts full of dirty bags.

"You'd be surprised," Pearl said drolly.

"Why is everyone staring at us?" Eve realized that as they walked, people were casting her odd glances.

"Because you are the only one they can see."

Crud. Her cheeks flamed. "Oh, so they all just think I'm talking to myself." Marvelous. Now *she* looked as crazy as the people she'd always thought were nuts.

Pearl dismissed her concerns with a wave of her hand. "It's Chicago, dear. Everybody does it." She paused as they continued walking. "And you are allowed to inspire, but not to lead."

"Uh-huh." Eve wasn't sure what that meant exactly, but she'd figure it out.

"And then you must do all of this by yourself," Pearl added. "You must find your own way, and under no circumstances are you to form any attachments or relationships." These words were delivered with heavy weight.

Eve glanced over at the angel as snow fell, chilling her cheeks and reminding her what it felt like to be alive. "Well, I never found time to do that on earth. I don't think I'm going to start in the afterlife." She smothered a sardonic chuckle, unable to do more than shake her head at herself. Truer words had never been spoken. Ah, well.

They paused, and Pearl eyed her hard. "And… no contacting anyone that you know."

Dusk fell quickly and bathed Chicago in darkness. The skyline was bright with smattered lights on the high-rise buildings. Life moved through the city in waves of sound, the honking of horns, the chatter of people, wandering to and fro as they made their way to wherever they were headed.

"I have fondness for this city," Pearl said from the park bench just outside downtown proper, where they looked at everything hustling and bustling before them. "I love to come back and check it out when I can." Despite the cold in the air, she didn't seem chilled at all, even clad in just her thin white garb. She pointed. "I grew up in Wicker Park."

"How long ago was that?"

Pearl retorted, "Let's just say I've been wearing white a long time."

That made Eve chuckle. She shook her head as she eyed the cityscape in fresh wonder. "I never noticed all the colors. The lights and the sounds. It's so beautiful."

Like a painting. How was it she'd never sat on a bench and just looked at the skyline?

Not taking her eyes off the view, Pearl whispered in response, "Yeah."

A thought came to Eve, and she felt a surge of sadness. "My brother... I have to tell my brother. He doesn't know what happened to me." Tyler must have so many questions.

"Yes, he does," Pearl said quickly. "You have to focus on your assignment now. You have a little girl who's extremely worried about her uncle. He's at a crossroads in his life, and I'm afraid he's lost his way."

Eve shook off thoughts of her brother. She'd deal with that. But first, she had to understand the details of her assignment. "Okay, but what am I supposed to do?" How could she possibly help with this?

Pearl sighed and stood. "I don't know how you're going to fix it, but you really need to do it before Christmas. Let's go."

Chapter Three

There was that strange sensation again as Pearl took Eve's hand, and then she found herself back in downtown Chicago, transported through time to the next day. It was probably lunchtime now, the crowd bustling around her. Snow fell in fat flakes as they walked toward a building bearing a sign that read Max's Diner.

"There he is," Pearl declared, leading Eve to the front door of the place.

Inside, a man was behind the diner's counter. He looked over at Eve, and their eyes connected.

Wait a minute. "Him?" Was Pearl serious? He was the musician she'd shared a cab with—she was certain of it. "But… I know him."

Pearl shook her head. "No, not really."

Eve heaved a sigh as her stomach flipped over itself. This guy was her assignment, the uncle who had lost his way, and she was supposed to help? "Pearl?" She glanced around and realized the angel was missing. "Pearl? Pearl?" she cried out, looking desperately up and down the sidewalk. "Come back!" She'd left without explaining what was next, and Eve felt her nerves clawing at her.

The diner door dinged open, and there was the man in question, standing in the doorway and staring at her, his brow quirked. "Did you... lose a reindeer or something?" he asked with a smirk.

Due to the confusion in her mind, Eve blurted out, "Uh... an angel." She winced internally at the words, knowing she sounded silly, and felt her cheeks explode in flames. *Smooth, Eve. Really smooth.*

His brow furrowed as he studied her. "'Hark-the-herald-angels-sing' angel?" Yeah, he definitely thought she was certifiable. Well, this was a fantastic start to her assignment.

"Fa-la-la-la-la, la-la-la-la?" she responded and plastered on a wide smile. Maybe he'd think it was a joke if she played it off like one.

That got him to laugh, his brown eyes sparkling. And something about that laugh made her feel warm inside. Maybe, just maybe, this assignment wasn't going to be so bad. She had to admit, he was charming when he wasn't trying to steal her cab.

"So, are you going to come in or just stand there and treat us to carols all day?" he asked, a lingering chuckle evident in his voice.

She lifted her head and eyed him. "Trust me, you don't want me singing."

The guy opened the door wider and welcomed her inside.

Delicious scents of food wafted right to her, and she sighed, her mouth watering in response. Could angels drink or eat? She hoped so, because she could destroy a piece of pie right now. Not to mention how much she wanted a coffee. Pearl hadn't exactly filled her in on these finer nuances of her new career. She made a mental note to ask the elusive angel next time she saw her.

The guy went back behind the counter, and Eve slipped onto a stool, resting her forearms on the smooth bar surface. Behind her, people chatted in booths as they ate lunch. Life was going on around her the same as before, though everything had changed for her.

"So," he said with a grin to Eve, crossing his arms over his chest. "Didn't think I'd see you again."

"Me neither," she admitted.

Wow, his eyes were quite brilliant when he smiled. She couldn't help but respond similarly.

"Maybe it's fate," he teased.

She jumped on the topic. This might be her in to figure out exactly what the crossroads issue was so she could come up with the strategy to help him. "Maybe, yeah. At this point, I think that I'd probably believe just about anything."

He nodded toward the door. "What was all that outside?"

She scrambled for a response to the question, then

decided she could give him the truth—at least, the partial truth. "I recently hit my head," she admitted.

"Are you all right?" he asked, concern clear in his voice, brows furrowed in a frown.

"I'm alive for now." Not really much else to say about that. She was still wrapping her head around this whole angel business. Yes, she'd grudgingly accepted it was true, but that didn't mean she had any idea what she was doing. And speaking of, time to get more information out of him so she could form her plan of action. She looked around the diner. "So, you work here."

"Manager, cook, bouncer, owner," he said glibly.

Oh, so was he the Max in the business name? "Where's your guitar?" she asked out of curiosity. Was that a side gig for him?

The light in his eyes dimmed a bit at her question, and she saw a change come over him, evident in the sudden tension in his frame. "I don't need that to flip burgers."

Hmm, seemed like a touchy subject to him. Perhaps this was part of the issue. She latched on to it and filed it away in her mind.

"So, what can I get you?" he asked, all business now.

"Uh, a triple espresso please."

"How about black coffee with unlimited refills?" he countered.

"I'll take it," she said with a laugh.

Max went over to the coffee station, chatting with

a blonde waitress. Eve took the time to look around at the people in the diner. The reality of her situation hit her, and she sighed. Her life—or whatever it was called now—was going to be changed permanently.

Part of her wanted to go back to her apartment, crawl under the sheets of her cozy bed, and hide out there while she tried to figure out how to adjust.

Eve was no quitter, though. Yeah, things hadn't gone according to her plan. But she would make the best of this situation. She just needed to remember that she was a go-getter—relentless, driven. She'd made deals happen when no one else had believed they were possible. Surely this wouldn't be *that* hard.

Determination helped her to steel her spine. Okay, this wasn't what she'd planned for herself, but she was going to help this man. Achieve her goals.

The guy brought the coffee to her, and her brain whirred as she came up with her pitch to him. Probably the guitar thing was part of the issue—it was clear from his reaction. Eve was good about listening to her gut. It was what made her so successful in her career. And it would serve her well in this one too.

"So, did you make your appointment on time?" she asked.

"No," he said lightly. "There was a traffic jam on Madison." With that, he gave her a knowing look.

Her stomach sank. "I'm sorry."

He didn't say anything as he put the coffeepot back in its place.

Time to start fixing things. Eve pasted on a smile

and slid into the long-familiar role. "Okay, you know what? I'm just gonna come right out and say it. Let the chips fall where they may."

He eyed her skeptically.

She pressed on, determined. "I can see that you have a lot going on here. But is your bottom line where you want it to be?"

The skeptical look in his eyes turned to utter confusion. He leaned forward. "Is my what what?"

"Priorities," she said, warming into her pitch. She could make him understand using the language of her business. The concept was universal. "You know, guitar, diner, diner, guitar." As she explained, she waved her hands like two scales moving back and forth. Surely he could see that his focuses weren't in balance.

"Still not following."

Okay, maybe she wasn't making it as clear as she thought she was. Her brain scrambled for a new approach. "I... I..." she struggled, then saw Pearl sitting on a stool several feet away, shaking her head at Eve. Boy, she was messing this up. She cleared her throat and turned her attention back to the guy. "I feel like maybe you are... at a crossroads."

Even without looking over at Pearl, she could tell the angel was rolling her eyes.

He stared at her in silence, then said, "You really should get that head checked." With that, he moved out from behind the counter, away from her and toward the door. "Sally, will you take this for me, please? I've gotta get Lauren home. Come on, kiddo—it's late."

As he walked away, Eve felt the disappointing rush of failure hitting her hard. Okay, so her typical strategy to win someone over to her line of thought wasn't going to work in this case. And the look on Pearl's face echoed that sentiment. Plus, he thought she was nuts. She was now even further back than when she'd started.

"By the way," Max said as he donned his coat. "I Googled partridges. They do go in trees."

"Pear trees?" she asked.

He eyed her in silence, then took a young girl's hand and led her outside.

"Can I get you anything else?" the blonde waitress asked Eve.

Eve sighed and rested her head on her hand, elbow propped on the table. "No, no, that's it. Thank you."

The door dinged as he and his niece left.

Well, that went badly.

"I'm going to need a new assignment," Eve declared to Pearl as they strolled down the sidewalk. The Christmas decorations were out in full force—trees laden with colorful ornaments, life-sized nutcrackers in bold red regalia standing tall around pillars, bright red poinsettias perched on every available surface. She could smell the rich scent of fresh-cut pine trees filling the air.

Even the people around them seemed in holiday

spirits, carrying bags bearing presents, clutching hot cups of coffee to ward off the chill, and laughing and talking with each other. It made her realize again how she was here but not really a part of things. Same as her life had been until the day she'd died.

"I think maybe... a new approach," Pearl retorted.

"He's probably out getting a restraining order right now," she complained. Man, she'd managed to screw up royally. How did angels do this?

Eve was a competent, strong, independent woman. A career woman, one who made lofty business goals and achieved them. But when it came to dealing with people, she was floundering, hard. She sighed.

"Since when would that even bother you?" Pearl teased.

"Just how much do you know about me?" she asked, looking over at the angel still clad in all white. Had Pearl been checking her out before all of this? She must have decided to recruit her for this task.

Pearl took a moment before answering. "I know that you are driven. People think that you're very relentless and ambitious."

"Is that what people think of me?" Why was it when Pearl said these things, they sounded more like negatives instead of positives? Her chest tightened in response.

"It is. They call you The Poacher."

The Poacher? That sounded awful—and lonely. Like a woman who had nothing to come home to each night except... "My cat!" she cried out, suddenly remembering poor Forbes. She was the worst pet caregiver ever. How could she not have thought about her kitty until now? Wow, nothing like feeling like a failure all around. "I forgot all about him. He's all alone."

Pearl gave a knowing shake of her head. "Come on, then. Let's go check on the cat so you can focus on your task." She took Eve's hand, and they shimmered then appeared in Eve's apartment.

It was evident that Ruth, who was standing in the kitchen holding Forbes, couldn't see them.

"So?" a maintenance man said to Ruth, walking toward her. "What happened?"

"She was in a terrible accident, and I haven't noticed anybody come by to look after him." The cat made a sound, and Ruth cooed, petting his fur. "Don't worry, Eve. I'll take care of Forbes. You like Christmas? You're going to love staying with me and Tinsel. Yes, you are," she said, bouncing the cat like a baby. They exited the apartment.

Eve stared in shock at the now-empty place. Her mind was reeling with what had just happened. "I just can't believe she would do that for me," she said to Pearl.

The angel looked around the apartment. "It's as if no one ever lived here."

But Eve wasn't paying much attention to what she was saying. "I mean… I hardly speak to her." Guilt weighed on her like a blanket, heavy and steady. The woman had always been nice to her whenever they'd met, and Eve had brushed her off. She'd barely made time to learn more than her name. And still, Ruth had taken the cat in without a second thought.

"Well, that's what neighbors are for, dear. You know, to help each other out." Pearl continued scouting around, eyeing everything in Eve's pristine apartment in thinly veiled surprise.

"I'm not sure that I would do the same," Eve admitted. Boy, being dead was forcing her to face a lot of her flaws. She wasn't liking the things she saw.

"Maybe this is your chance to redeem yourself," Pearl pointed out. Her gaze landed on a picture frame on the counter, and she picked it up. "Oh, who are these people?"

"Uh, I don't know. They were just in the frame when I bought it. I never had a chance to put a picture in there." She'd liked the frame and had meant to put one of the boys in. But of course, given how busy she was, she hadn't gotten around to it.

Pearl's eyes were wide, like she couldn't believe what she was hearing. "Really?"

Embarrassment flooded Eve's cheeks. "Yeah." That did sound strange now that she said it out loud. Who couldn't take thirty seconds to slip a picture into a frame? Someone who didn't really look around her, that was who.

Pearl meandered over to the fridge and opened it, eyeing the rows of bottled water and nonfat yogurt. "Why, there's no food."

"I ate out a lot," Eve said, suddenly feeling

defensive. Having this angel walking around in her apartment, pointing out these things… Okay, so yeah, she hadn't made this place feel like a home since she'd moved in. But who had time for that when there was a lot of important work to be done? Eve decided to change the subject off her life and back onto the task at hand. There was a job to do. "So how does this really even work? What do I do? Where do I go?"

"You can go anywhere you want," Pearl said.

"Do I sleep?"

"You know the old adage 'you'll sleep when you're dead?'"

Eve nodded.

"That's not true," Pearl said succinctly.

"Oh." Well, that answered that. Not that she'd felt tired, but what was she going to do at night? Wander around the city? Sit in bed and read? It wasn't like there were books on how to be a successful angel or classes she could take to advance herself. Were there? She shook her head at her strange line of thought. "Do I eat?"

"You can eat anything you want. You'll never put on weight."

Okay, maybe this angel gig wasn't so bad, after all. At least there was one perk. "Wow." She mulled the whole thing over. "And you actually think that I can change someone's life?" That was the real question on her mind, the one that was gnawing at her.

Eve could make big deals happen for their investment firm. But when it came to personal interaction with people, she fell flat, as was evidenced earlier today in the diner. She always thought there would be time later to handle those things, for her to develop relationships and intimate connections. How was she supposed to forge an intimate connection with Max to bring about his niece's Christmas wish?

"I absolutely do," Pearl said, no trace of uncertainty in her voice.

The words humbled her. "Why?" she asked quietly.

Pearl looked at her. "Well, you picked stock, and I pick people, and I picked you." Plain truths, delivered in a plain fashion.

Eve swallowed. The enormity of her task was starting to settle in. Christmas wasn't too far away. But Pearl believed in her, and she wasn't going to let anyone down—not the angel, not the guy, and not his niece.

Eve might not be the best choice for the job, but she wasn't going to back down from the challenge.

The door dinged as Lauren came into the diner, followed by her grandparents. She greeted Max, the waitress, Sally, and Joe, a regular who practically lived there. He shifted his burly frame on the stool and spun around to face her.

"Where have you been at, girl?" he asked with a toothy smile. "We've got a yo-yo lesson." He showed her a move called walk the reindeer—not to be confused with walk the dog, mind you.

Max smiled at Lauren's grandmother, Marla, as he bussed dirty dishes off a table. "You guys have fun?"

"Yeah, we took her shopping. We got her some things for the warmer weather."

He frowned at the implication of her words, his chest tightening. He knew where this conversation was going, how she would push him, and he wasn't ready for it. "You didn't tell her, did you?"

"No. But somebody needs to."

The light accusation in her voice grated at him. "You don't have to keep reminding me, Marla."

"Apparently, I do. She spends four nights a week in a diner, and that is no place for a little girl. You're just making it worse by waiting."

Max sighed and turned to the woman. "How can it possibly be worse?" he said in a low tone, glancing over at Lauren. Her parents were dead, and she was living with a man who couldn't seem to get himself together.

He didn't want to have this conversation right now. He knew what he needed to do, but the dread of Lauren's reaction had kept him silent. He moved around the woman and headed toward the back of the kitchen with the dirty plates.

Time was ticking away. Christmas was almost here, and then New Year's, and then Lauren would be going to live in the south with her grandparents. Now he just had to tell her. It was the best move for her, he reminded himself as he dropped the dishes into the sink.

Even still, knowing that didn't make it any easier for him to sit down and explain it.

Eve stepped into the diner, smiling at the cozy atmosphere. The blonde waitress—Sally, according to her tag—nodded at her.

"Back for a refill?" she asked.

"Yes, please," Eve declared, settling onto the stool at the end of the counter. She glanced over to see the niece at a stool farther down, a piece of cake in front of her papers, which were spread out on the counter. "And, um, I'll have whatever she's having."

"Hmm, angel food."

That got Eve's attention. Her throat grew tight. "What?" Could Sally have guessed that she wasn't actually human?

"She means my cake," the girl said in a knowing tone, tossing her long hair back.

"Oh." Thank goodness. The tension eased in her. She wasn't busted. "Yes, yes. And, um, some pie."

"Apple or cherry?" Sally asked.

"Both?" Hey, she was going to take advantage of the positives of being an angel as much as possible. How long had it been since she'd eaten anything dessert-like other than nonfat yogurt? Pitiful. Time to live large, so to speak.

The girl side-eyed her. "Did a boy just break up with you? I've heard older kids talk about how they like to eat their feelings when they're sad—whatever that means."

Eve laughed and reached for her freshly poured coffee. "No."

"Then why are you ordering three desserts?"

"Well…" Eve spun on the stool and turned to the girl, whispering, "I just found out that I can eat whatever I want and not gain weight."

The girl grinned. "Me too!" They shared a moment of solidarity, then she said, "I'm Lauren."

"Hi, I'm Eve."

"Like… Christmas Eve."

"That's right, yes," she said with a nod. How ironic to be a Christmas angel named Eve. She shook her head, wondering if that was fate, too. She looked at the papers in Lauren's hand. "Whatcha working on?"

"School play," she said, a frown marring her brow. "It's tonight, and I don't have the lines down."

"Uh-oh," Eve said with a smile. She remembered those days well, the panic of standing on a stage and not feeling prepared. Poor thing. She moved to the free stool between her and Lauren. "Hmm. Oh. 'Hark, ye shepherds, cometh thy flock in joy.' Yikes!" That was a mouthful. No wonder the girl was worried. Sally brought over the desserts, and Eve turned her attention to the woman. "Wow, thank you. Do you have a pen I can borrow?"

"Yeah."

She took the offered pen from Sally and told Lauren, "Okay, so I have this memory trick. I use it to remember clients' information." Well, *used*, but that was neither here nor there. This trick should help the girl. She began scrawling on the side of the paper. "So you take each letter from the beginning and you say, 'Hey, you sharks… cover… that… fellow… in… jam!' Each letter corresponds to your line. Do you wanna try?"

Lauren nodded. "'Hark, ye shepherds, cometh thy flock in joy.'" She gasped and gave a grin so wide that it made Eve grin widely in return. "I did it!" She looked over Eve's shoulder. "Uncle Max, I did it!"

"You did so good!" Eve enthused with the girl.

Uncle Max clapped and stepped over to them, and Eve found her heart giving a funny little skip at the sight of his crooked smile aimed at her. "Thanks," he said to Eve. "Cake and pie and… pie are on the house." Wisely, he didn't say anything about how much she was eating.

She gave him a gracious 'thank you' and began to dig into the angel food cake. It was light and fluffy and better than she'd imagined it would be. When was the last time she'd had this kind of a treat? Childhood? She and Tyler used to have contests to see who could eat the most in one sitting. Their mom would get so mad when she came home and saw the pie she'd just made the night before completely gone.

Lauren got up to talk to someone at a booth.

Eve finished chewing the delicious bite, pushing away painful thoughts of her brother, then looked up at Max. "Um… we kind of got off to a rough start. I apologize."

"Apology accepted." And now it was his turn to be gracious.

"Okay." There, she felt better. At least she'd done something good for Lauren, and she had dessert. Surely this was a good starting place for her job. Not that she knew exactly what would happen to her if she failed making the girl's Christmas wish come true. Pearl hadn't exactly been forthcoming on those details.

But that didn't matter. She *wouldn't* fail—Eve was driven and successful, thrived under pressure, and excelled at accomplishing tasks. She would get this done, of course, and done well… even if helping people in such a personal manner wasn't exactly her typical kind of success.

"You live around here?" He interrupted her musings, coming around the corner of the counter.

She took another massive bite of cake. Oh wow, it was… heavenly. Pun intended. "I'm… in the process of relocating," she said generically. "You must be the favorite uncle."

"That's me," he said as he grabbed more dirty dishes.

"Are her parents on holiday?"

He paused, and she could practically see the mood shift around him. "No," he said in a quiet tone. "They're, um…" He sat down two stools away from her. "They were in an accident," he continued, leaning toward her. "Going on two years now. Her mom was my sister."

Eve felt a deep sadness welling in her. "That's terrible," she breathed. He nodded. "I'm sorry." What a difficult situation.

"They made me guardian if anything should happen. I just, uh... never thought it would." She could see the weight in his eyes, the heaviness of missing his sister and caring for his niece.

What could she say? She'd never known that kind of pain. But her heart hurt for him—for them both. Before she could say anything, Lauren came bouncing over.

"Can Eve come to my school play tonight?" the girl asked her uncle.

Max gave an awkward laugh. "She's probably busy, sweetie."

He was trying to give her an out. A nice gesture. But this would be a perfect chance for her to work more on her assignment, giving her an opportunity to pick his brain and find out why he wasn't playing music anymore. Not to mention the fact that she was honored the girl wanted her there. "I would love to 'cometh'," she declared to Lauren.

"You... do realize that it's a fifth-grade Christmas play," he said drolly.

"Yes! Where is that theatrical event happening?" she asked them.

"Grover Cleveland Elementary on 17th."

She knew that school. Had been to it herself a

couple of times, in fact. "Do you… do you happen to know these brothers, Bobby and Caleb Morgan?" she asked Lauren on impulse.

"Yeah," the girl said. "They were supposed to be shepherds in our play. They had some sort of family emergency."

Eve stilled for a moment. She knew what that emergency was.

Sally pulled Lauren away to help with something in the kitchen, and Eve sat deep in thought. Her nephews. How much she missed them. The last time she'd seen them had been far too brief—a rushed meeting before a conference call. She wished she could see the boys, hug them. Hear their laughs again.

Max pulled her out of her sad thoughts and leaned a bit closer to her with a crooked grin. "Maybe we should exchange numbers. You know, in case critics close the play early."

Oh, good idea—it would make it easier for her to interact with him. She reached into her pocket for her ever-present phone… only to belatedly remember that she didn't have a phone anymore. Or a purse. Or a living identity. *Crud.* "I… I lost my phone," she fumbled.

His brows quirked. "You lost—"

"Yeah, I should go." Eve stood. She was feeling a bit overwhelmed and needed to recollect herself before the play tonight. To wrap her head around this situation and come up with a game plan. But before she could do that, she had to go see her family. Check on them, see how they were dealing with her death. Feel their presence once more.

"Oh. Sure." His words seemed distracted, but she barely noticed.

"Thank you," Eve tossed over her shoulder, then bundled up and darted out into the brisk December air.

Chapter Four

E ve and Pearl materialized on the stairwell in Tyler's house. Christmas garland laden with red and white ornaments was strung along the handrails. The rich scent of cranberry spice candles filled the air. Tyler and Sherry always decorated their home for the holidays, and this year was evidently no exception.

Downstairs, Caleb and Bobby were sitting at the table in silence, coloring on paper.

"They can't hear you or see you," Pearl reminded her. Eve had begged the angel to let her check on her family; thankfully, Pearl had acquiesced, saying she'd allow it just this once to help Eve let go and move on. "This is what we call 'gazing.' It's the guardian angel's way of looking in on those we love."

Did Pearl do this for anyone in her life?

Before she could ask, her brother appeared. "Hey, guys," Tyler said, entering the dining room, his wife behind him. "What are you doing?"

"Making pictures for Aunt Eve," Bobby said in a hushed tone. The bounce he usually had was gone, and in its place was a boy Eve barely recognized.

"So she can be here with us," Caleb added. "Even when she can't be."

"She'd love both of these," Tyler said as Sherry rubbed Caleb's back. "I know it."

"The last time I saw him," Eve said to Pearl, "I blew him off for a client." Shame filled her—shame, guilt, and regret. Her chest ached with the emotions flooding her. "I just... I can't let that be the last thing between us." The argument they'd had, when he'd accused her of being a workaholic... He'd been so right. And now she couldn't fix it.

"Don't break the rules," Pearl warned.

"I just want to tell him I'm sorry." She watched the family in silence. "I missed so much. All their soccer games and trick-or-treating and, of course, Christmas." And for what? She'd died, and now all those chances were gone. She'd lost her opportunities to get closer to them, to be a bigger part of their lives.

What would they remember about her? What a workaholic she was? How her company had sent them fruit baskets for Christmas? *Ugh*. So many mistakes. So many embarrassing mistakes. She'd fumbled everything with them when she'd been alive, and now she couldn't make amends. It was too late. What she wouldn't give to go back and change things. To do it all right. To show them she loved them, come to their house this Christmas and hug them all so tightly.

"Don't you think maybe you're too hard on yourself?" Pearl asked.

"For their birthday, I got them a gift card, and then I had my assistant sign it," she admitted, mortification filling her chest.

"That *is* lame," Pearl said, nodding. "Come on. Nothing more to see here. We gotta go. You have an assignment to work on."

Eve wanted to linger, to watch her brother and Sherry and the boys as long as she could. But Pearl was right. Max needed her. Lauren needed her. And while she couldn't do anything to repair her relationships with her family, she could do this. Somehow.

She drew in a deep breath and said, "You're right. Okay, I'm ready to go."

It was only mid-afternoon, so Eve decided to kill some time walking around Chicago before the play that night. The sun shone brightly overhead, giving a little warmth to the briskness in the air. Eve strolled up and down the streets, watching clusters of people with their families and friends. She'd lived downtown for years but had never meandered the city. Never took in the sights. Viewed them through a fresh lens of someone who was finally awake for the first time, ironically.

Being without her phone glued to her hand gave her a new perspective on the world around her. Was it always this pretty during the holidays? The decorations and the joyousness in the air made her steps feel lighter.

Eve had never really cared much about Christmas, not since she was a kid. She'd piled on the responsibilities, and the season had become less and less important. Just another holiday that came and went. But now that this was possibly her last Christmas to celebrate on earth, she found she wanted to savor the experience as much as possible. Take it in, enjoy it the way she never had before.

Have some memories to bring back to heaven when she had to leave earth.

She watched as kids oohed and aahed at the displays in the windows. A man dressed as Santa rang a bell and offered cheer to everyone around him.

The sight of him reminded her of Carter and that silly Santa hat he'd had on the last time she'd seen him, when he'd brought her eggnog at the office. What was going on there with her work? She felt a pull, that old, familiar urge to go back to her desk, to see how her clients were dealing with her being gone. Who was handling the workload now?

She shook her head at her impulse. All that effort she'd put in year after year, the long hours, and for what?

She should have stepped away from her desk and gone to the office holiday party that night. Mingled and talked. How much did she really know about any of her coworkers? Or even about Liz, her assistant? She only knew as much as she needed to get her work done and make the big deals.

Eve sighed. Carter had told her he was once like her. Had he had some major revelation that had changed him? Made him less about work and more about... life?

And why had she never cared about it before? About him, about Ruth, about Tyler and Sherry and the kids, about anyone or anything other than her career aspirations? Yes, she loved her family, but she'd never shown them. Not the way they deserved.

She felt uncomfortable, like her skin was too tight. Everything that had seemed important when she'd been alive suddenly didn't matter anymore. The clients she'd schmoozed, all the meaningless, minute details she'd memorized about their families to impress them—none of it had been for any purpose other than the bottom line. To make money.

Money, career, fancy apartment—that stuff wasn't relevant now. Maybe had never been, if she was honest with herself. And boy, was she learning that lesson the hard way. Too bad it was too late.

"You're going to do great, kiddo," Max declared as he led Lauren back.

"Make sure to save a seat for Eve," she reminded him, so certain that the woman was going to show up.

"I will," he promised and waved her off. She filed

in with the other kids, all dressed in their costumes, chatting about how nervous they were.

Max padded his way down the hall toward the auditorium, thinking about Eve. What a strange woman she was. She said the weirdest stuff. And yet, he found himself intrigued by her. Her mesmerizing eyes, the way her whole face lit up when she smiled.

He found his seat beside Marla and Ben, saving one for Eve in a likely futile effort. Minutes passed by as Marla talked about Lauren's costume and the holiday shopping they still had to do. The dark auditorium filled with parents and family members.

Max glanced at his watch yet again—the play was going to start any minute now. And she wasn't here.

He bit back a sarcastic laugh. Did he really expect Eve to show up after that excuse she gave regarding having no phone? He recognized a brush-off when he heard it. And she'd given him a good one. He'd been a fool to think otherwise. She was just a random woman he'd run into a couple of times, that was all. Best to put her out of his mind.

Marla shifted in her seat beside him. She probably noticed him looking at his watch every minute but wisely didn't say a word.

"Excuse me, excuse me," a soft voice said as heels lightly pattered up the aisle. Eve was there, a smile on her pretty face, beaming down at Max as she slipped into the empty seat beside him.

She'd come.

His pulse kicked up, and he couldn't help his responding grin.

"Hi," she said breathlessly. Cold from the outside poured off her, and even in the dark, he could see her flushed cheeks.

"You made it." He knew how dumb that sounded—obviously she had. She was right here. But still, he'd been so sure she wasn't actually going to come. All those thoughts had been swept away by her presence.

"Of course!" She nudged a lock of dark hair off her brow.

"You really did lose your phone." Guess it hadn't been a line after all.

She nodded. "Yes, I did."

Manners. He had them. He shook his head at himself and introduced Eve to the row of attendees—Lauren's dad's parents, Marla and Ben, Sally, and Joe. She gave them all friendly smiles and waves.

Then the lights went up, and a boy donned in a brown robe stepped out onstage. "In the town of Bethlehem, on a starry night, a baby was born."

A girl came out to stand beside him. "And three wise men followed a star to the ma-ma-manger," she stuttered. "To ce-ce-celebrate its joyous celebration."

Eve gave an empathetic chuckle beside him, and he found himself doing it, too. Having her here suddenly made things feel different. Better. She seemed genuinely interested in what was going on onstage.

And then Lauren was up there, and he straightened.

Eve did, too. Something in him warmed at the way she appeared vested in this, despite barely knowing them.

"Hark, ye shepherds cometh, their flock in joy," Lauren declared in a bold tone.

Max beamed. Eve beamed. They shared a look between them, and suddenly, he was aware of her physical presence beside him. The way her arm brushed against his. The soft intakes of her breath. How her dark eyes lit from within. She was pretty.

Very pretty.

When was the last time he'd thought about anything other than work or his failed musical career? It had been a while. But this woman was a breath of fresh air, and he found himself wondering more about her story. Maybe when the play was over, she'd hang out with him for a little while. He wanted to spend more time with her.

The rest of the students got onstage and recited their lines, some fumbling the words, some doing great. It was cute, and hearing Eve's pleased sounds made it even more enjoyable. When the play was done, their group lingered in the auditorium waiting for Lauren to come to them.

She ran, jumping into his arms for a huge hug. "Uncle Max!"

"Kiddo!" he said, kissing her on the head. "You were amazing."

"Thanks." She turned toward the woman who'd occupied far too much of Max's thoughts tonight. "That was because of Eve."

"No," she protested, her cheeks stained with a delicate flush, "it was all you!"

"I tried to teach your trick to the other shepherds, but it didn't go so well." She shrugged.

"Yeah, we noticed," Joe said, and everyone laughed.

While Lauren chattered with Sally about the play and how the others had done, Marla took Eve by the arm and led her away. "Well, I'm glad that Max won't be alone, at least," she said, beaming at Eve.

"Oh, no," she said. "We just met." The woman was getting the wrong idea about them, though Eve had to admit, she did feel an attraction to him. Pearl had warned her not to make attachments, though, and she planned to adhere to that. It's just business, she reminded herself.

"Oh, he must like you. He invited you to Lauren's play." There was a definite knowing spark in the woman's eyes that Eve didn't miss, her crow's lines deepening with her smile.

"No, Lauren invited me," she said with a dismissive wave.

"Well, maybe you can talk some sense into him," Marla said, one hand clutching the playbook. "He needs to tell her."

Eve shook her head, clueless. What was Marla talking about?

"She's coming to live with us after the new year."

Lauren? "Where do you live?"

"Florida," the woman declared as her husband came over to join them. Eve reeled—Lauren was moving away from Chicago, from the home she'd known for the past two years? "We have a lovely house with a pool, and there are kids her age everywhere," Marla continued. "It's a wonderful place to grow up."

"But don't you think she'll miss Max?" Was it a good idea to uproot Lauren from her home when she so clearly loved Max?

"Well, he can visit," Marla pointed out.

"Come on, Marla, you've said enough," Ben said, wrapping an arm around her shoulders and guiding her away.

Ben told the group that he and Marla were going to take Lauren to see Santa. Lauren, of course, was excited about the prospect.

Max hugged the little girl as Eve watched, still trying to process what she'd been told. Lauren didn't even know she was moving. How was she going to feel about this big change? And did Max want this—was that why he hadn't told her yet, because he was holding off? Could this be part of the crossroads he was at? The problem seemed more complicated than Eve had originally thought.

"Good night, kiddo," he said, kissing Lauren's head again.

"See you later," she replied, hugging him and pulling back.

He offered his fist, and she bumped it. "Not unless I see you first."

Lauren turned to Eve and gave her a hug, and she

felt something in her chest melt at the gesture. "We did it."

"You were wonderful," she said, pressing a kiss to her brow.

Lauren left, and then they were alone.

"She is so amazing," Eve gushed.

"Yeah, she is." There was no mistaking the love in Max's eyes when he talked about his niece. They both drew in deep breaths and chuckled. "So, I'm guessing you don't have a Christmas tree."

"You are right."

He shook his head in mock pity. "That will not stand."

"What?" she said in equally mock shock.

He waved at her, and she couldn't resist the invitation. "Come with me."

Chapter Five

E ve and Max walked a couple of blocks down the road. Snow was falling in beautiful, fluffy clumps, and their breaths puffed in front of them. Eve kept stealing glances at Max. Something about him drew her closer, made her want to be around him.

He's just a job, she warned herself. Pearl had told her not to get attached, and she intended to remember that. Though it was hard when she got faint whiffs of his cologne, the spices teasing her nostrils.

And when he moved, his arm brushed against hers, and even with the coats between them, she felt herself shivering. The cold wasn't to blame.

Just a job. An admittedly attractive job, but that was all.

They rounded the corner, and she saw a Christmas tree lot. The whole place was lit up with bright lights that glittered in the dark, casting a warm glow on the trees waiting for homes for the holiday. It was enchanting, and she gasped in surprise.

"This is beautiful," she said, breathing in the scent of fresh-cut trees.

Max cupped her elbow to lead her there, and she fought the urge to lean closer to him. "Check it out—over here they have wreaths."

"Wow," she said in awe, moving away from him to step toward one wreath in particular. "This wreath is exactly like the one my brother and I always had when we were kids." Memories of times long ago slammed into her. Their family had been so poor, but they always looked forward to getting their Christmas wreath—it had helped their small home feel more festive.

It was a tradition they'd stopped doing once they'd become adults and had started earning money of their own. Tyler bought trees now, and she... Well, she didn't do anything. A sense of loss filled her, and she shook it off. This wasn't the time for sadness. Max had brought her somewhere beautiful, and she intended to enjoy it.

"Yeah, we never had a tree, but we always had a wreath," she continued.

"You put your presents under a wreath?" he asked.

"Well," she said lightly, "there weren't very many of those." She shrugged and took the wreath into her hands. "I always promised myself that I would never be poor." A promise she'd kept, that was for sure. "And I thought that there'd be time for the perfect

Christmas later." And now, here she was, unable to enjoy her earnings.

"So, maybe this is later," he offered.

She glanced over at his friendly smile, and her heart skipped. *Just a job. Just a job.* He was so inviting to be around, though. And the way he looked at her made her think that maybe that spark wasn't one-sided.

"Hey, Max," a bearded man clad in thick winter gear said in a jovial tone.

"Hey, buddy!" Max said, shaking his hand.

"About time you brought a girlfriend here," the guy teased him.

Eve felt her cheeks burn in response. She looked away and put the wreath on a nearby table. Snow speckled the greenery.

"Hey, that's enough," Max said with a laugh. "This is Eve. We just met."

"Hi," she said to the guy.

He began to sing. "You're... together now, together—"

"Okay, thank you," Max said, cutting him off.

"Best song he ever wrote," the man declared.

"Just sell me a wreath, please?" Max said, thrusting a handful of cash at the guy.

"Wait!" Eve said as recognition hit her. She stared in wonder at Max. "'Together now?' That does sound familiar."

"You must have seen him sing it on TV," the guy said. "He and his sister won *America's Got Music.*"

"That was a long time ago," Max said in a low voice.

"A couple of years is nothing," the man declared.

Max shook his head. "It's a lifetime." He walked away, his shoulders hunched. It was clear the conversation bothered him. But it was illuminating for Eve, who was beginning to get a better picture. No wonder Lauren had made a Christmas wish for her uncle. Max's life had been turned upside down—not just by the death of his sister, but the loss of his musical career.

She had to help him.

With a polite smile, Eve thanked the man for ringing up their purchase and took the wreath to follow Max.

They meandered down the sidewalk. Now that it was dark, the lights covering the bare trees lining the walkway were glowing. Garland was hung everywhere with fat red bows, and trees were decorated with shining bulbs. Downtown Chicago looked incredible, and Eve couldn't stop staring at the decorations.

Max, ever the gentleman, took the wreath to carry and moved in silence, seemingly unaffected by the holiday spirit surrounding them, and Eve wondered what he was thinking. She could sense emotions rolling off him, and part of her longed to wrap him in a big, comforting hug. Was that crossing the line? Would he even welcome a hug?

"I have a question for you," she started. "You know the night that I met you in the cab? Where were you going?"

"An audition," he admitted.

Guilt hit her again, swift and heavy. Was this whole ordeal partly her fault? With her insistence that her meeting was more important? "Oh, did I make you miss it?"

He shook his head, giving her a comforting smile. "Oh, it's no big deal. It was just some Christmas Eve thing."

"Wait, downtown?"

"The Palace?"

She gasped. "I made you miss a show at The Palace? I feel terrible!" How was she going to fix this for him?

"Don't," he said with a wry smile. "I wasn't really that late. I only agreed to go because Lauren kept bugging me, and when I got there, I... just couldn't do it."

"I don't understand."

They walked in silence for a moment as he seemed to gather his thoughts. Then he said, "My sister Becky and I were a team. We wrote together, we sang together, since we were kids." The words seemed dragged out of him. "Then we finally got a record deal from that show. Something we used to dream about." He sounded wistful now, sad, and Eve's heart went out to him.

He shifted the wreath on his arm. "We went out to celebrate that night. Tod and Becky left early. The streets were icy." Oh, she knew where this was going. She drew her lower lip between her teeth. "Car went off the road."

She found herself reaching over to stroke his arm, a touch of solidarity.

"Music didn't seem so… important after that," he said with a shrug. "Label dropped me, end of story."

The mood was somber and quiet between them for a moment as she processed what he was saying. What a tragedy. Poor Max.

"I'm so sorry," she offered. After another moment of silence, she glanced up at the sky and saw the snowflakes falling, light sparkling off their surfaces. It looked enchanting, like she was in a snow globe. She slowed to a stop and stared around her in wide-eyed wonder. "It's so beautiful," she breathed.

He eyed her with a touch of skepticism. "You have seen snow before, right?"

"Yes, of course," she said sheepishly. "I think I just… never really took the time to appreciate it." It was like she was seeing everything fresh. The world had so much beauty in it, even when it had tragedy. So many things she hadn't noticed when she was alive. So many wasted hours sitting in her office and not really living.

Max's eyes connected with hers, and she felt her heart give a little stutter at the intimacy of the moment. Him sharing this with her was significant somehow. She knew this job was about him, but she felt like part of her was changing, too.

"You know, I live just up the street," he said. "If you wanna come sit by the fire." Out of nowhere, Pearl materialized behind him, arms crossed, staring hard at Eve. "My fireplace is fake," he continued with a chuckle, "but we can sit by the radiator."

Disapproval oozed from Pearl; Eve was surprised Max couldn't feel it heating his back. She gave a small laugh. Point noted, she thought. This was on the no-no list. "I've got to go."

He looked disappointed but covered it fast. "Oh, okay. I'll call you a cab."

"No, no," she protested. "I'm good."

"Don't forget this," he said, passing the wreath to her.

"Oh, right!" Their fingers brushed, and she simultaneously wanted to move closer and run away. This was so bad. "Thank you. I had a really great time," she told him, hoping the truth of her words came across.

"Me too," he said quietly.

Pearl shook her head in warning, and Eve took that as her cue to go. She spun on her heels.

"Oh," Max said, snagging her attention. "Lauren and I are putting together meals for the needy tomorrow. It's kind of a holiday tradition we have." He thrust his hands into his coat pockets.

"That's lovely," she told him. With purposeful intent, she ignored Pearl, keeping her focus on Max.

"It's... also a holiday tradition to invite someone you just met in a cab."

She couldn't help it. A smile broke out on her face. "Really?"

He chuckled. "No. But I think I'm going to start that one."

"When and where?" she found herself asking. Her pulse sped up in anticipation of seeing him again.

"Noon?" he suggested, and then Pearl swept by him and reached over to grab Eve's arm, spinning her back around. "All Saints'... on Park?"

"I'll be there!" she said over her shoulder as Pearl dragged her down the street. She gave him a wide smile.

Pearl materialized them into Max's Diner, which was closed for the night. Christmas lights twinkled outside icy windows and created a colorful glow. They took a seat at the counter, and Eve prepared herself for the inquisition.

"What did I say about not getting involved?" the angel started.

Eve sighed. "But how am I supposed to help if I don't get involved?" It was a genuine question, but it also deflected the truth—she was maybe, sorta, kinda developing a crush on Max.

"You've been doing it your whole life," Pearl retorted.

Low blow, but honest. She sighed. "Oh, I just wish I'd met him when I was alive."

"You did." Two words, delivered plainly, hit their mark.

Early the next morning, Tyler's front door opened, and he stepped outside onto the porch. Eve watched from a distance to see what his reaction would be when he saw it.

After a pause, he picked the wreath up that she'd propped against his house and eyed it. Even from where she stood, she could spot the emotion welling in his eyes. He peered around the neighborhood, probably to find the person who'd left it. But he wouldn't be able to see her—Pearl had made sure of that.

Tyler stepped inside, and Eve noticed Sherry walk toward him, a questioning look on her face as he showed her the wreath.

"Where did you get that?" she asked him.

"Didn't you buy it?"

"No," Sherry answered.

Eve smiled and pressed her hand against the tree beside her. I miss you, Tyler, she thought. And while she couldn't be with him, she wanted him to have this memory again, one that had been so important to them as kids.

"It was on the porch," Tyler explained to his wife.

"It's beautiful," she said, reaching over to touch a red ribbon.

"It's exactly like the one Eve and I had when we were kids." Tyler's voice was hushed as he spoke.

She'd known he'd remember. Hopefully, when he hung it up, he'd think of her. And he'd know that even though she had passed on, she'd always be in his memories.

With a sad smile, Eve walked away.

Max sat in his living room, guitar perched on

his leg. He strummed a chord. Lyrics began to well in him out of nowhere. "The fire is warm," he sang, then strummed again and let the words flow. Yes, that would work. He put the guitar pick in his mouth and scrawled the lyrics and chords down on the sheet.

This morning, he'd woken up inspired and feeling better than he had in ages. The soft glow of morning filled the apartment with light, and he'd left Lauren sleeping in her room to creep into the living room and give in to this momentary flash of motivation.

It might not last, but he wanted to take advantage of the spark while it was there.

He knew what the cause of this sudden change was. Eve.

Last night, he'd shared his painful story with her, and she'd opened up to him about her past, too. He couldn't remember the last time he'd been this drawn to a woman. What was it about her that seemed... otherworldly in a way? Like she was special.

As he wrote down the next chord, Lauren padded over to him and rested her arms on the table, her hair sleep-mussed.

"Hey!" he said to her. "What are you doing up so early?"

"I heard music," she said with a smile.

"Really?" he teased, and then positioned his fingers back on the strings. "You must have been dreaming."

"You like her, don't you?"

He glanced over his shoulder at her inquisitive stare. The kid saw too much. He murmured a generic response and flipped the sheet music over. "Come on. What do you want for breakfast?" He put the guitar down and got up, and Lauren followed him.

She settled in at the kitchen table and flipped her hair back behind her. "So you're not going to talk about it?"

"There's nothing to talk about," he murmured and grabbed a box of cereal, two bowls and spoons, and the milk, poured them both a hefty amount, then settled one in front of her. Lauren was rabid for cereal and could eat almost as much as him, which never ceased to amuse him.

"Uncle Max," she said, one brow quirked. "I'm not dumb, you know. I can see by the way you look at her."

He narrowed his eyes. "See what?"

"That you like her." Lauren rolled her eyes in a *duh* fashion. "She's awesome. I like her too. And I like that you're playing music again."

"Don't get ahead of yourself, kiddo," he warned, scooping a large bite into his mouth and chewing on the sugary goodness. Lauren did the same. After he swallowed, he continued. "I was just fiddling around."

But the truth was, he wasn't just fiddling around. The song had welled up in him, and he'd had to get it out. Even now, it was spinning in his head, begging to be released. The chords were taunting him, asking him to run back to the guitar and get it down on paper.

It had been so long since he'd had this feeling. Could he trust it? What if it went away and he was left with a half-finished, useless song? The fear was real.

But the impulse to create was stronger.

"You ready for today?" he asked, ruffling her hair.

She beamed. "I already picked out my clothes. Did Eve say she's coming?"

He frowned. "How did you know I asked her?"

There was that *duh* look again, the one that was so like how his sister eyed him that he couldn't help but chuckle. "Uncle Max. Really?"

He stood and pressed a kiss to her head. "You're too much, kiddo." He left the kitchen.

"Wear your dark green sweater," she hollered at his retreating back. "It looks good on you."

He smirked and shook his head.

Chapter Six

Eve walked through the empty corridor of Crestlane. It was so weird being back here after days of not working. The urge had finally caught up to her, and she'd given in and gone to visit the place that had been her second home. Well, first home really. So much time she'd spent in this building, so many hours sitting at her desk.

The office was closed for the holiday, so no one was there to pay any attention to her as she strolled across the carpeted floor. The overhead lights were all dimmed to save on electricity. She made her way toward her office, curiosity urging her steps a little faster. What had happened to all her clients? She would just take a little peek around to see where they'd been distributed. Had Carter been assigned any of them?

When she got to her office, she saw Liz, wearing a pale gray pencil skirt and black dress shirt, holding her office phone and smiling. Eve's list of potential clients were on the computer screen in front of her.

"Hi there, this is Liz with Crestlane Financial. I'll be temporarily taking over Eve Morgan's accounts. Please call me anytime, day or night—including Christmas—and I'll be happy to help. Thank you so much for your time." Liz hung up the phone.

Eve shook her head with a wry smile. "You little poacher." She'd learned from the best, though. Eve herself had demonstrated some of those same tricks.

Liz grabbed her jacket off the back of the office chair and left the room. Of course, she couldn't see Eve, who was invisible. When the woman was gone, Eve materialized herself into the room and looked around at the place she'd basically lived in through a new lens. So sterile, just like her apartment. Like her life.

She had one personal artifact there that showed the existence of a real person—a picture of her brother and his family. Eve picked up the photo and clutched it, smiling at the shot. She should have plastered the office with pictures the way Carter had. His office showed a life well lived.

She couldn't change the past, but she could make sure anyone else who entered the office knew who was important to her. She moved the photo to a prominent spot on her desk.

So strange to be back here. She'd only been gone a few days, but everything had changed. This place didn't feel like it had before. It didn't feel like home.

What was life going to be like after this assignment was done? Would she be whisked back up to heaven and sit around playing the harp or something? Would Pearl give her another assignment? Or was this a one-and-done kind of deal?

So many questions she still didn't have answers to. So many regrets.

Eve left the building and made her way toward the church where she was meeting Max and Lauren. The sun was warm, and pristine white snow covered the trees in a thick blanket. It was a lovely walk.

She thrust her hands into the pockets of her red coat and enjoyed the view.

As an angel, she didn't get tired. She could walk endlessly and never feel fatigued. Much nicer than taking stuffy cabs everywhere. And this way, she could see more of Chicago. After all, she didn't know when she was going to be here again, and she wanted to absorb everything she could.

Her heart gave a funny pang at the thought, and she pressed her lips together. No time to think about that right now. There would be time enough later. Today, she was going to enjoy the day.

Eve watched kids scoop up wads of snow and fling them at each other, hollering and laughing during the impromptu snowball fight. She and Tyler used to do the same—some things never changed.

As she got to the sidewalk in front of the church, her stomach began to flutter madly. Was she nervous?

It had to be about the job, right? Not because of the prospect of seeing Max again.

Max exited the front doors, dumping a bag of garbage into the can. When he saw her, he smiled, and that flutter in her stomach turned into a mass of butterflies. "Hey," he said, clearly happy to see her, too.

"Hey," she replied back.

To ward off the chill in the air, he tucked his hands under his arms, since he didn't have on a coat. "You showed up."

"Of course I showed up," she said with a laugh. "I wasn't going to miss this for the world."

He hustled over to her. "Come inside. Let me show you what we've got going on." He touched her arm to nudge her toward the door, and her darn cheeks burst into heat at the gesture. She knew he didn't mean anything by it, so why was she reacting this way?

When they entered the church, she heard the sounds of the choir singing a Christmas song. They were clad in dark blue robes with light blue accents, hymnals perched in their hands. The director stood in front and waved merrily in rhythm.

The two of them walked over to the station where Lauren was stacking rolls in a bowl, and Max picked up a knife and resumed chopping vegetables. When she saw Eve, her smile was genuine, and Eve beamed back. "I'm so glad you came, Eve," she said warmly.

Eve reached over and touched the girl's shoulder. "Me too. This is amazing."

Max nodded toward the big pot he was filling. "My famous Christmas chili."

"My mom taught him how to cook," Lauren explained.

"Really?" Eve grinned at Max.

"She figured I should have some life skills in case the whole music thing didn't work out," he said dryly as he chopped more. "Come on," he said and moved a knife toward her. "Grab an onion."

"Okay, but I warn you, my brother tried to teach me to cook one time and it didn't take."

"Duly noted," he said in a mock serious tone. He scooped more veggies into the pot. "You guys close?"

"You know, we were when we were little. We were best friends." She shook her head. "And then, somehow, I just started putting everything else first."

"I'm sure you're not that bad," he said, clearly trying to soothe her guilt.

"Trust me," she said as she hacked into the onion. "After cancelling last year for the *third* Christmas in a row, I spent the holiday at my desk eating chicken salad."

"Well, nothing says Christmas like chicken salad," he teased. The way his eyes looked at her as he talked, like she had his full attention… it was hypnotic. She couldn't help but respond to it. "It's what the wise men ate." At her laugh, he added, "They don't include that in the songs, but it's true."

As they talked, Lauren looked on in interest.

Max heaved a sigh and wiped his shirt sleeve across

his eye—no doubt a reaction to the onions she was cutting. "At least you have the rest of your life to make up for it, huh?"

That made Eve still. "Yeah," she murmured. What could she tell him, that she'd missed her chance and blew it? She wasn't allowed to let him know the truth. No one could know. With that realization, a sudden wave of loneliness hit her.

She'd brought this on herself, she knew it, but that didn't stop the longing she had for connection. Being with Max and Lauren these last few days had made her realize just how much she'd missed out on—with her brother and his family, and with others.

Max's eyes watered, and he squinted at her. "How are you not crying?"

"Uh… I'm crying on the inside," she offered. Not exactly like she could explain that angels didn't cry. Pearl would throw a fit.

"All right," he said, but he didn't look convinced.

They finished preparing the chili like a well-oiled machine. As they set it to simmer, Lauren chattered on, telling stories about when Max took her ice skating and wiped out on the ice. She cackled as she described the sight of him going bottom-first, feet up in the air.

Max shook his head and sighed, but he shot an indulgent smile at the girl.

It was clear that he loved her. So why was he letting her move to Florida with her grandparents? Didn't he think she'd be happy with him? Eve watched the two of them, mulling over the issues.

First, she needed to help him get back into music. Second, she wanted him to see how important he was to Lauren and reconsider sending her away.

Lofty goals, indeed.

"So, what do you think?" Lauren asked Eve.

She blinked. Apparently, she'd missed something, given the way the two of them were looking at her. "Um, sorry. Spaced out for a second. Probably time for more coffee." She grinned at the girl. "What did you say?"

"I asked if you'd come help us decorate our tree," she repeated. "We have all the ornaments ready, and we're gonna make hot cocoa, and Uncle Max has the best marshmallows for them."

Part of Eve knew she was treading on dangerous ground. She was starting to feel attached to this little family. But she had to get close if she was going to help. Maybe she could use the opportunity to ask more questions. She gave Max a coy glance. "Are you sure that's okay? I don't want to intrude."

He didn't say anything at first, just reached over and took her hand. "We'd love to have you," he said quietly. The feel of his hand in hers made her lower belly begin its mad flutters once more.

With a request like that, how could she say no?

Soft piano Christmas music played in the background of Max's living room. Surprisingly, it didn't irritate Eve the way it used to. Maybe it was because she didn't want this Christmas season to end. She was enjoying her time on earth, trying to stretch the days as long as possible. And the music added to the ambiance of the holiday.

"You have to put the heavier ornaments on the bigger branches," Lauren explained to Eve as she put a white glass ball on the tree.

"Ah, why didn't I think of that?" Eve ducked down and hung her green ball lower.

"You'll catch on," the girl said in a sage tone.

Eve chuckled.

They finished putting the ornaments on, then Lauren declared, "Now, the most important thing is the angel on top."

"Wait, wait," Max said as he came into the room. "That's my domain. Uncle Max territory. Come here," he said, leaning down to take the angel and crawling on a nearby chair. "Ready? Here we go."

Once the angel was perched on the top, they all applauded.

Eve couldn't remember the last time she'd decorated a tree. Her heart was full and yet light, and she felt giddy. Why hadn't she done this more? Tyler had invited her over to help him and the boys, but she'd always declined. Always too busy.

A pang of sadness hit her at yet another missed opportunity.

Well, at least she was here now, and she was beginning to understand. There was some comfort in that, though not a lot.

"Oh, wait, wait," Max said, stepping down. "The

piece de resistance. You ready?" He ducked down to plug the tree in. "And... one, two, three!"

The tree lit up, and the beautiful work they'd done chased away the sadness. It was enchanting. She hugged Lauren to her.

"It's perfect," the girl said, eyes wide. "Isn't it, Eve?"

"Yes," she said with a nod. "It's perfect."

"Well," Max said with a glance at his watch. "I hate to be that guy. Time for bed, kiddo. It's late."

"Can Eve read me a bedtime story?" she asked, giving her a pleading look.

"Lauren," Max said in a warning tone.

"There's nothing I'd rather do," Eve answered.

Once Lauren was dressed in her pajamas and tucked into bed, Eve entered the room and saw the girl clutching a picture frame on her lap. She sat down on the bed beside her, holding *The Night Before Christmas*, and peered at the photo.

"That's my mom and dad," Lauren explained. "They're in heaven now." Sadness filled her voice.

"You look just like them," Eve said gently.

"Somedays, I feel like they're still here. Like they're watching over me." The words were spoken almost as if an admission. Poor thing. She had to miss them terribly.

"I'm sure that they are."

"Really?" Some of the earlier sadness lifted in her eyes.

"Yes. Every time that you think about your mom and your dad, they're right here with you."

"You mean... inside? In my heart?"

"Yeah," she whispered. Of course, there was a chance they were angels, too, able to come down and check on her regularly. But there was no way to explain that to her. "Forever."

Lauren seemed comforted by the thought and snuggled into her bed.

"All right," Eve said as she took the picture frame and put it on the dresser. "You ready?" With the girl's nod, she began to read. "'Twas the night before Christmas, and all through the house, not a creature was stirring, not even a mouse."

The girl gave a contented smile and let her eyes drift closed as she listened. Eve couldn't remember the last time she'd felt so cozy, so grounded in the moment—not thinking of the future, but living in the present. And heaven help her, she didn't want this to end.

When Lauren was fast asleep, Eve dropped a kiss on her forehead and slipped out of the room. Max was pouring two glasses of white wine.

"Hey, you know we're having a little Christmas party at the diner tomorrow night," he said with a smile. "You should come."

"Yeah," she said, chuckling under her breath. "Lauren already invited me." It had been the last thing she'd said before drifting off to sleep. There was no way Eve could refuse her. "Also, we're going to build a snowman in the morning, if that's okay with you."

Max walked over, bearing both glasses of wine. He

handed her one, not taking his eyes off her. Eve felt her pulse thrumming in her neck at the intensity of his gaze. What was he thinking?

He tilted his head and scrutinized her, leaning back to rest against the dining room table. "You know, when we met in the cab, you were in such a rush, and now it seems like you've got all the time in the world."

Crud. Eve sighed and glanced away, sipping her wine. She hadn't thought about what she'd say if he started questioning her hanging around so much. "I wish that were true," she admitted. Christmas was just around the corner. She was almost out of time. The days were passing too fast.

He paused. Straightened. "What are you not telling me?"

The man was far too astute. Was she going to confess that she was an angel sent to help make Lauren's wish come true for Christmas, and that she'd then vanish back to heaven likely forever? Right. He'd check her into a mental institution. "Nothing," she replied in a light tone.

He raised his brows. Clearly, he didn't believe her.

"It's... complicated," she hedged.

"What? Witness protection?"

"I wish." She laughed and walked over to the tree to put some space between her and him. He saw way too much, and she had to keep her distance. She couldn't let herself slide into fantasizing about things that would never be—a life on earth where she had more time with him.

He came up behind her and put his glass on the table. "Please tell me you are not in a relationship."

She closed her eyes and shook her head. "No, no. I'm in nothing." The words came out more bitter than she meant.

"Eve," he started. She could feel him so close, his presence soothing, inviting. She turned around and noted his furrowed brow. He was worried—about her. The realization made her heart squeeze for a long, painful second. "Are... you dying?"

"No," she answered on a hard exhale. "That, I'm not."

"Then what is it?"

Oh, how she wanted to confide in him. He was wise, funny, empathetic. And it had been so long since she'd dropped her guard and let someone in. Since she'd even made time to spend with someone, in fact. Max was an incredible man—and she couldn't open up to him. "Could you just trust me for now?"

He sighed and gave a brief nod. "Okay." He scooped up his glass. "I'll trust you." She could tell he wasn't enthused, but he was willing to give this to her. To know she had his trust moved her. "You'll tell me one day, right?"

"One day," she said with a nod, knowing that was false but wishing it was true. "You know, I should probably be going," she said, uneasy. Things were getting too personal with them. And she wanted it, wanted this to be something it wasn't. She needed to pull back and get a breath of fresh air, get him out of her head. This was far too dangerous.

"Wait, what? It's early." He looked at his watch.

"Oh, really?" she said with a smile and grabbed her coat. "You just told Lauren it was late."

"Lauren is nine," he countered. But he relented. "I'll walk you out."

They exited the building and stood under the overhang.

Max glanced up, giving a small smirk. "I hate to bombard you with too much Christmas…" He laughed and pointed up.

Mistletoe. Eve chuckled, as well, even though she felt a flush crawl up her cheeks and across her chest, and not from the warmth of her coat.

Max stepped closer. Eve could smell his cologne, a fresh scent that drew her to him. "You know," he said jovially, "there's an old holiday custom."

"I have heard of it," she said on a chuckle.

His gaze caught on her lips, and she found herself leaning toward him, pulse erratic, breath caught in her throat. A kiss. Just one kiss.

A small clump of snow splattered on their heads, and Eve squealed in surprise. Snow dusted their hair and faces. She blinked and wiped it away, laughing.

"Hey, how's that for timing?" he asked dryly, looking up. He scruffed the snow off his head, straightened, then looked at her again with that heart-stopping gaze. "Where were we?"

They leaned toward each other again, their mouths mere inches apart.

Another mass of snow dumped on them. Eve

looked up… and saw Pearl staring down, disapproval etched on her face. Okay, well, that answered that.

"Guess it's not my day," he murmured and worked to clear more snow off him.

Pearl waved her finger in warning at Eve.

"Um," Eve said to Max, "I've really got to go." He tried to protest, but she squeezed his hands and repeated, "I've got to go." Then she fled down the sidewalk.

Chapter Seven

T he Chicago skyline sparkled in the dark night. Eve stood by Pearl on the dock near the river. Cool breezes wafted off the water, fluttering their hair. Another brisk night as Christmas inched closer and closer.

She glared at Pearl, frustration filling her chest. "It wouldn't have killed you to let me have that kiss. It might be the last one I ever get." That much was true, but she knew that wasn't what made her irritated right now. It was that she wanted the kiss with *Max*. But he was her job and thus, off-limits in Pearl's eyes. Who came up with these rules, anyway?

"Don't blame me for all those wasted years," Pearl lobbed back. The hit was perfectly aimed, lodging square in Eve's chest.

She drew her lip between her teeth and eyed the angel. "I have three more days. At least let me have them." She knew she was pleading, asking for something she probably couldn't be given, but the stakes were too high for her to pull back now.

Pearl dropped her voice. "I'm trying to spare you an afterlife of heartbreak."

"What?"

The angel shrugged, her tone ringing with genuine regret. "He's not going to remember you anyway."

The words made Eve uneasy. "What do you mean?" Yeah, she knew it hadn't been that long, but she was pretty sure she'd made an impression on him—and on Lauren. She knew they'd made one on her.

Pearl gave a heavy sigh. "I mean that the changes that you make down here, they will stay." She paused. "But the memory of you? Won't."

Eve's stomach turned over itself. It couldn't be true. Why was she just now hearing this? Irritation at this information being kept from her welled up. "Max and Lauren won't remember anything about me?"

Pearl looked her in the eyes, shaking her head, and Eve realized how serious this Christmas angel business was. It wasn't for the fainthearted. Part of her wished she'd never been picked for this assignment. "It will be as though you never existed."

Disappointment and frustration filled Eve's chest, and she couldn't speak. The last few days had been wonderful, the best she'd had in so, so long. And to know, after her time was up with them, they wouldn't remember her? It stung. Deeply.

"This is why I've warned you not to get attached," Pearl added. "I hate to see you get hurt when they move forward and live their lives without you. Your job is to help them do that, and letting your heart get in the way will only leave you damaged, not them."

Pearl left her alone to think about what she'd revealed.

Eve spent hours wandering around the city in the dark, her heart heavy, chin tucked into her scarf as she stared dully ahead at the ground. Would she have approached things with Max and Lauren differently had she known that catch? *Could* she have kept her distance?

Eve sighed and plopped down onto the bench where she'd sat with Pearl the first night she'd come back down to earth. She stared blindly at the cityscape, but for the first time in days, it brought no pleasure, no joy. How could it, when she felt like she was losing everything? Again.

The pain of realizing she'd died now seemed to get even bigger as she understood that she was really, truly gone. No more a part of this earth. Her chest was tight, her throat squeezed, and still, she couldn't cry, even though she wanted to.

Yet another reminder she wasn't human.

Her mind cycled through the last few days with Max. How he made her feel. The way he smiled at her, his surprise at seeing her when she'd shown up at the school play.

Walking with him when they got the wreath and seeing the snow—really seeing it—for the first time.

Their honest conversation and the way they'd gotten to know each other...

Curling up beside Lauren and reading to her, watching the little girl fall asleep and wishing she could experience that again somehow.

And then back to the beginning, when she'd first met Max, the confusion over whose cab it was. How even then she'd found herself attracted to him, though she'd refused to give it any credence. No, she'd been too busy focusing on work to look around her and realize what had been in front of her.

Story of her life.

Mere days had passed since she'd hit her head in that fatal accident, but the length of time didn't matter.

Her eyes had been opened. She'd found, with Max and Lauren, something she'd been missing for years. And there was no hope for her, no chance to make that a reality. How quickly she'd forgotten as she'd let herself get caught up in her fantasy—in the magic she'd seen in Max's eyes.

Was he thinking about her now? She shouldn't want him to, but she did. She wanted these next three days to etch themselves into her heart, even if he'd never remember it. Because she would, and she'd carry those feelings with her.

Three days. So little time to accomplish huge things. Eve had to think bigger, had to get things moving soon before she ran out of time. The clock was ticking, but the deadline brought with it a double sense of dread now that she knew what was waiting for her after.

A long stretch of eternity without these two people she'd grown to care for.

The next morning, Eve and Pearl stood in her kitchen in front of an open laptop, watching Max and his sister perform on an episode of *America's Got Music*. Eve absorbed the scene before her, noted the energy the two siblings had together, the sheer joy in Max's eyes as he sang and played his guitar.

Music was his passion. And she had to help him find it again.

She forced herself to view things dispassionately, not through the eyes of someone who was developing inappropriate feelings for the man. There was no place for that right now.

Instead, she let the music carry her. Listened to the uproar of the audience when they finished performing. Everyone loved them.

"They were so good," she breathed.

"They were," Pearl agreed.

Eve sighed, closed the window browser, and looked away from the laptop. "He's given up his music, and now, he's going to give up Lauren. This is not what his sister would have wanted." The woman and her husband had bestowed guardianship upon him for a reason. They knew he'd take care of the little girl the best. "I mean, I wouldn't want my brother to give up everything he loved just because I—" Eve paused when she realized what she was about to say. "Died."

Pearl gave her a sad, knowing look. It was clear the angel felt for her, even though she was the one handing down the rules.

Her frustration was overwhelming. Everything felt messed up, and she wanted things to be right— including her own botched-up life. She hopped up onto the countertop. "I would do it all so differently if I had a second chance," she admitted.

Pearl said, "I hear that a lot."

"I just don't know how I lost track of everything that was important." Why had she been so blind? Now she was dead, and it couldn't be fixed.

"I hear that a lot, too," Pearl said wryly.

"You must hear everything a lot." What would it be like to be in the angel's place? To see those who'd passed and were given jobs as angels have to face the reality of what they'd flubbed when they'd been alive? The regrets people had that they couldn't seem to let go of?

"Well, one thing I never hear..." Pearl stopped and closed her eyes for a moment, and the weight of what she was about to say struck Eve hard. "No one has ever said, 'I spent too much time loving someone.'"

Eve couldn't help the slow exhale that slid from her. If only she'd listened to her brother. To Carter. To anyone who'd tried to tell her to slow down, enjoy life. To pursue what really mattered, not just work and obligations.

She was extra determined to accomplish her deed. To help Max understand what a blessing he had in Lauren and in his passion for music. Because before he knew it, he might be in her situation one day, regretting not giving those things he loved the chance they deserved.

She refused to let that happen. Max and Lauren meant too much to her. She wouldn't fail them.

Three days, including today. Miracles could be done in that length of time, right?

Eve slid down off the counter and lifted her chin, then eyed Pearl. "Well, I've faced bad odds before and came out victorious." She wasn't going to back down or give up. She was driven, purposeful, and this time, it was over something that mattered.

Eve had a snowman to make with Lauren, and then tonight, she was going to the diner's Christmas party. Possible ideas were brewing in her head on how to fix the situation. She just needed to face the challenge instead of thinking it was hopeless.

Nothing was hopeless so long as she was still here.

Eve walked through the door of the diner and smiled at the scene before her. The entire place was decked out in Christmas decorations. Lights were strung all over, lending an intimate glow to the interior. Music was playing, and a couple of people danced.

Eve slid out of her coat and put it aside, revealing her red dress. She kept her gift bag in her hand. "Hey," she said when she saw Max in his usual spot behind the counter. He looked muscular and attractive in a pale gray sweater and dark jeans.

When his gaze turned to hers, her pulse didn't pay her any attention and began an erratic beat, despite her willing herself to not give in to the sensation. "Hey," he said brightly as he came over to her. "You look…" He glanced up and down, and she flushed with pleasure at the appreciation in his eyes. "Wow."

She suddenly felt vulnerable. "Really? It's not too Christmas-y?"

"You can never be too…" Max stopped talking when Sally the waitress strolled between the two of them, noshing on a cookie. The woman was wearing a jingly Santa hat paired with a red Christmas sweater that probably should have stayed in the back of the dresser. He raised a brow. "I take it back," he confided to Eve. "You can be too Christmas-y."

She laughed and held up her bag. "I brought you some gifts."

"That is so sweet. Hey, Lauren, look who's here!" He turned his attention back to Eve. "We've got some for you, too."

As he darted to the back, Lauren came over and hugged Eve. Eve planted a kiss on Lauren's head, glad to see her. The girl had on an adorable dress covered in candy canes.

"Oh, you didn't have to do that," Eve protested

when Max came back, presenting her with a bright green gift bag.

"Open it!" Lauren insisted.

"Okay." She dug beneath the red tissue paper and saw what they'd gotten her. Despite her earlier self-warnings about not getting too soft with him, her heart melted. "A pre-paid phone with ninety free minutes. That's exactly what I needed. Thank you."

Max nodded with a slight smile on his face, and Eve couldn't help but stare into those deep, dark eyes. He wanted to be able to reach her—that much was evident by the gift. And she only had two full days left after tonight. Not enough time, her heart cried out.

"I put Uncle Max on your speed dial," Lauren said with a toothy grin.

"Really? What number?" she asked.

"Two," Max said with a shrug.

"Aww," she teased. "Not number one?"

"He said we shouldn't be presumptuous," Lauren answered.

Eve took the girl's hand and led her to a booth. They sat down. "I got you a present. But what I really want to tell you is that you are the gift that makes your Uncle Max happy." She hoped Lauren could feel the sincerity coming from her. Lauren was a wonderful child, and she needed to know that she was important and loved. "You're the only gift that he needs. And I want you to remember that always." Knowing that Lauren wouldn't remember her in a couple of days made her emphasize this last point.

She wouldn't be around to say it. She hoped the emotion would linger after she was gone.

Eve's heart sank, but she shook the feeling off and forced a smile. "No matter what happens, even if you forget everything else. Even if you forget me."

"I could never forget you, Eve." She spoke with such earnestness that it touched Eve. But she knew the truth.

"Great party, Max." The booming voice came from Ben, Lauren's grandfather, as he stood near the entrance of the diner, wearing his coat. Marla was beside him.

Max ripped his attention off Eve, who seemed to glow tonight, and turned to the door. "You guys leaving already?"

"We're headed back to the hotel. Ben's tired."

He eyed Ben, who didn't look all that fatigued.

Marla leaned in. "I hope you're not having second thoughts. Because we agreed this is what's best for her."

Max peered over at Lauren, at her beaming face as she talked to her friends in the diner. "I'm pretty sure *you* agreed."

"We can give her the kind of life that she needs." The same argument Marla had been making since the topic came up. "That she deserves." She paused, shrugged her coat on a little tighter. "Do the right thing."

Ben nodded. "See you tomorrow." And with that, the two of them left.

Max turned back to the party and saw Eve looking at him, concern in her eyes. Time to change the subject from the one nagging at his brain. "So, where were we?"

Eve opened her mouth then paused. She glanced down, then back up at him. He frowned, knowing she was about to say something important. "This is none of my business," she started, "but sending Lauren to live with her grandparents? Is that really the right thing?"

So she'd overheard the conversation. He swallowed, then looked away. "I don't know," he admitted. He'd thought it was. After all, what use was he to Lauren? Just a music hack who wasn't good for anything but flipping burgers. Still... "The thought of not seeing her every day... it kills me." He eyed Lauren, who was blissfully unaware of what was going on. "She's the most important thing in my life. But..." He paused, then shrugged. "They can give her a real home, you know?"

"But this is her home." Eve said it so simply, like that was all there was to it.

"This is a diner," he corrected.

Her eyes softened. "No, this is where her family is. This is where *you* are." She reached out and touched his upper arm, and he felt the emotion pouring off her. She really cared about Lauren—about him. "I mean, look at all these people who love her. And she's happy."

When Lauren saw Eve gazing at her, she hopped

up and came over. "Eve, come see the cookies I made with Sally and Joe!"

Eve stepped over to the plate and looked at the brightly decorated cookies. "Oh, wow."

"That one's yours," Lauren declared as she pointed to the cookie on the top. "It's an angel."

"Oh, I love it!" Eve said.

Lauren peered up at her then seemed to freeze. What was wrong? She glanced at the top of Eve's head, her mouth parting in surprise. "You really are an angel."

"What?" What was she talking about? How could she possibly know? Eve's heart kicked hard against her ribcage.

"Look." Lauren pointed over her head. "You have a halo."

Eve glanced up. Oh, my. What was going on here? Where had this come from? Her brain scrambled for an explanation. "That's... just a reflection."

Lauren gave a wink and a nod, clearly not buying it. She leaned in. "Your secret's safe with me." She bounced away.

Eve couldn't help but laugh. She supposed there was no harm in the girl thinking so. The cell phone in her hand began to ring, and she answered it with a smile. "Hello?"

Max's inviting voice filled her ear, and she wanted to close her eyes and listen to him. "Do you dance?" She knew he was in the diner, but to keep the ruse going, she kept facing where she was, giving in to the moment.

"Well, it's been a long time," she confessed.

"Me too."

A slow Christmas song began playing. She finally looked around the room and saw him, propped up against the desserts cooler, cell phone pressed to his ear. He crooked a finger in her direction, and her pulse stuttered in response.

They hung up and moved to stand in front of each other. His scent, familiar and tempting, danced around her, drawing her closer. Those compelling eyes of his were locked on hers, and she felt herself sinking in, forgetting those things that had plagued her all day.

He reached out and took her hand, then led her toward a free spot and pressed her to him. His arms were comforting, wrapped around her, and she couldn't help but slide a hand up his shoulder to stroke his back.

She was unable to think. To speak. They swayed closer until their heads were scant inches apart. She could feel his breath brushing against her ear, and she closed her eyes, moving with him.

This was real magic, right here.

The hand holding hers clenched a fraction tighter, and his thumb stroked her skin. Her whole body grew warm and tingly, and she couldn't help the small sigh that escaped. He rested his cheek on her brow, and she sank into the embrace. Into the music. Into the moment.

Max. He was sweeping her away, and she felt light, free. Like for the first time in her life, she could breathe. Feel. Know what it meant to be alive.

The night ended far too soon. The party started to wind down, and Eve helped Max clean up after the last guests left. Lauren was curled up in a booth under a soft blanket, sleeping soundly.

Time to go.

Eve knew she had let herself get carried away, but she couldn't bring herself to regret it. Being with Max like that, dancing with him, had felt so right. She'd probably hear an earful from Pearl, but she'd cross that bridge later.

For now, though, she had to tell Max good night.

Eve donned her coat and Max escorted her out the door. They stood under the overhang, and she was reminded of the last time they'd done that.

He must have thought about it, too, because he glanced up. "Well, I don't see any snow drifts."

She laughed. "No, me neither."

The moment crackled between them, the energy from before coming back to life. And then Max was touching her waist, tugging her to him, and his mouth was on hers.

Eve's heart throbbed in response to the gentle caress of his lips. She slid her fingers up his shoulders, touching the soft hairs at the base of his neck. He reached his hands up and buried them in her hair, and they kissed in earnest.

The perfect ending to the perfect night.

A horn honked right in front of them, and Eve reluctantly pulled away from Max. She glanced over at the cab to see the back window rolling down. Sure enough, Pearl was there, her face unreadable.

"That was…" Max started.

"Yeah," she breathed. She gave his face a lingering stroke, not wanting to leave.

The horn honked again.

She practically floated to the taxi, unable to stop the smile on her face. "I feel so alive," she whispered to herself as she opened the door. Whatever Pearl was going to say in chastisement couldn't possibly dim the happiness in her right now. She was determined to hold on to this feeling, to that one perfect moment, for as long as she could.

Chapter Eight

Eve and Pearl whisked off to what Eve was beginning to think of as their meeting place—the bench outside the city. She knew she was still smiling from that night, could feel the weight of Pearl's gaze on her. But right now, it didn't matter.

Her heart was happy and full. And she couldn't remember the last time she'd experienced this.

"Look at you," Pearl finally said in a droll tone. "You're on cloud nine."

Eve laughed.

The angel rolled her eyes and shook her head like Eve was hopeless. "For goodness sake, I never should have let you have that kiss."

Her grin widened as she eyed Pearl. "It was pretty amazing." Amazing wasn't a big enough word to describe it. Spectacular. Earth-shattering. Memorable.

At least, for her.

No, she wasn't going to focus on what would come

later. She was going to relish the now, something she hadn't done enough of before.

"Yeah, well don't forget why you're here."

"Of course," she said with a nod. "I have two days and a plan." Before the diner, she'd spent the afternoon coming up with her strategy. It was going to work. It had to.

Pearl drew in a slow breath and stared out at the skyline. Seconds stretched in easy silence—it was clear she wasn't going to make Eve feel bad. "I'll never forget the first time my husband kissed me," she murmured, her tone wistful.

The thought of the angel married sparked curiosity in Eve. She wanted to know more about Pearl—how she'd gotten here, what had happened. "How long were you married for?"

"Thirty-five years, and every year was good."

"Wow." She paused to think that over. So many Christmases with the person you loved. What would that be like? In that moment, she envied Pearl. If only she'd done things differently. Had found a partner. "Is he in heaven with you?" Did they get to spend any time together?

Pearl glanced over. "No, he's in Wicker Park in our apartment."

Ah, it made sense now. "So that's why you like to come back to Chicago." Her husband was still here, living. She missed the man.

"I like to check in on him now and then, make

sure he refuses the casseroles of the woman next door." Her words were delivered in a staccato manner.

"Ah," she replied, wisely deciding to not offer an opinion on the topic.

"She's not right for him, you know," Pearl declared, eyeing Eve.

Eve nodded. "Okay."

Her phone rang. Eve couldn't help the little gasp that slipped out. She knew who it had to be. With a smile in her voice, she answered, "Hi," and chose to deliberately ignore Pearl's eye-rolling glare right before she disappeared from the bench.

"Hey," Max said. She closed her eyes and imagined him at home near the Christmas tree they'd all decorated together. "I was just thinking about you."

"Oh, really?"

"Yeah, I Googled 'people who don't cry when they cut onions.'"

"And what did you find?" she asked coyly.

"Zero results."

Surprise. Not exactly a human trait, was it? "Then I must just be very, very rare," she said smoothly.

"To put it mildly."

She could hear the warmth in his voice, and it made her heart stutter. Max had been thinking about her, even though she'd just seen him not an hour ago. He was feeling something, too.

"What are you doing?" he asked.

She exhaled and looked up into the dark sky. There were a few stars speckling the blackness. It was quiet and brisk, and she relished the feeling of being outside, something she hadn't done nearly enough of when alive. "I was thinking about life," she answered honestly.

"That sounds pretty serious," he murmured.

She glanced at her cell phone screen. "Did you know that I have eighty-seven minutes left on this phone?"

"That's crazy," he breathed. "I just happened to have exactly eighty-seven minutes free."

This man was going to leave an imprint on her heart that she'd never be able to erase. She was already in such big trouble. How was he so charming? He'd managed to capture her attention in a way she'd tried but failed to resist. "Where are you?" she found herself asking him.

"On the chair near the tree. You?"

She imagined him stretched out, the cozy lights twinkling and filling the room, bouncing off his face and brightening his eyes. Suddenly, Eve wanted to be there with him. But since she couldn't, she made herself vanish and reappear in her apartment, clad in pajamas. She slid onto her couch with a sigh and tossed a throw blanket over her lap. "On my couch."

"Describe your place to me," he asked. "I want to learn more about you."

Eve eyed her surroundings. What could she say that wouldn't make her sound like a total workaholic dud? There was nothing personal in here. "Well," she began, gnawing on her lower lip, "I live in an apartment. It has big windows and granite countertops."

"Did you hang up that wreath?" he asked.

"No," she said with a laugh. "I gave it to my brother. I figured he'd appreciate it. Kind of a gesture to reach out to him."

"There's hope for you, you know," Max said softly. "It's not too late to bridge the gap."

She closed her eyes and leaned her head back, exhaling. If only he knew. "I want to know more about *you*," she said to change the subject. "When did you start playing music?" Part of her plan was to get him reminiscing about the past and remember how it felt to embrace his passion. Then she'd present him with the second part of the plan that would clinch the deal.

There was a long pause, and she feared he would shy away from answering. Was she pressing him too hard? He finally said, "As far back as I can remember. My parents said I used to beat on the pots and pans. Needless to say, given that I demonstrated my musical aptitude before five in the morning, they weren't pleased."

She laughed, thinking about him toddling around, clanging everything in sight. "So you were a drummer?"

"They steered me toward guitar," he replied. "And it was love." She could hear the emotion in his voice as he talked. "My sister and I would hide away for hours, writing songs and practicing. We were so sure we would make it big. All we had to do was try and never give up." He sighed.

"So what made you audition for the show?" she asked in an effort to keep the conversation from turning sad.

"Becky hounded me about it until I relented," he admitted with a chuckle. "I didn't want to go. Had a case of stage fright. But she threatened to set my guitar on fire if I didn't give in."

"She sounds like she was tough," Eve said, shocked.

"She knew I needed a fire lit under me—metaphorically," he added in a wry tone. "I didn't want to test the boundaries and see if she'd literally do it." He paused. "So what do you do when you're not attending school plays or stealing cabs from total strangers?"

Her lips quirked. "I'm… in consulting." It was kind of true, a loose description of her job. "It's a rather new career path for me, to be honest. I worked for a large company dealing with stocks." A lucrative endeavor that had paid for this apartment outright. Her home for the next two nights until she was taken back up. She felt some kind of pang in her chest, one she couldn't quite identify.

Would she miss this place? Hmm, she wasn't sure. She would miss it if she'd bothered to put more of herself in here. But she'd been too busy worrying about it being functional over welcoming. Maybe more accurately, the pain she felt was nostalgia for this place because she hadn't appreciated it, hadn't made the most of what she'd had.

"I can see that," he mused, interrupting her thoughts. "You seem like someone who is a go-getter."

"I have my moments." She laughed.

"The tree looks great. Have you ever considered a career in Christmas tree decoration? Could prove to be worthwhile," he teased.

"I'm afraid the seasonal-help thing isn't for me," she admitted, thinking about the deadline she was facing. Christmas was two days away, and then her time would be up.

No more Max. No more Lauren.

No more Tyler or Sherry or the boys.

Everything was going to change.

When she'd first started this, she'd been excited for the unexpected chance to be in Chicago again. But now that she was here, really living for the first time since she was a kid, it pained her to face the reality of letting all of this go for good.

How had Max come to mean so much to her in such a short time?

"You know," he said in a low voice, "I wish you were here with me right now, sitting by the tree."

"I do too," she admitted. His house felt like a home, unlike hers. He had pictures and decorations, a life built there over the years. Not a sterile environment that barely counted as a residence.

If she could do it all again, she'd make a real home. She'd have her family over all the time, put the boys' drawings on her fridge. And she'd plaster their images everywhere to remind her what was really important.

Her heart grew heavy, and she lay down, stretching out on the couch, resting the phone against her ear.

Her minutes were growing shorter. Her days were almost up. And all she felt was an impending sense of loss.

After they hung up, Max sighed and put his phone on the coffee table. Somehow, in just a few days, Eve had wormed her way into his life, and she was dangerously close to worming her way into his heart. How was this possible?

Did it even matter? She was here, and she was breathing new life into him—a sort of muse.

Lyrics flowed through him as he thought about her, about what this Christmas was starting to mean for him. The impact she was having on him, how she helped him see everything through a new light. The last two years, he'd survived in a daze after his sister's death—getting by, working, taking care of Lauren—but he hadn't *felt*.

Hadn't really lived.

Eve shook everything up and opened his eyes. She was kind, caring, and she looked at him like he mattered.

Max grabbed his guitar, his song in progress, and a pencil. He strummed. Wrote. Strummed more. It was flowing through him in a way he hadn't felt in years, since before they'd begun auditioning in earnest. Back when it was just about the energy of the song.

Time slipped by; he didn't know how long he'd kept at it. Eventually, he found himself growing groggy.

Hands nudging him drew him out of deep sleep. "Uncle Max," a light voice said.

He snapped awake, realizing he was clenching the sheet music in his hand. His guitar was on his lap, as well. Fatigue still held him in its grip.

He sighed. "Hi."

"Were you up all night?" Lauren asked.

"I… I might have been," he replied, blinking and trying to wake up. The last thing he remembered was the piece he was working on—the one inspired by Eve.

Lauren slid off the side of the chair. "I made you coffee."

That made him perk up. "Really?" He put the music down and took the mug. "Thank you," he said warmly.

"Milk, five sugars," she declared, pride evident in her voice.

Oh, man. This coffee was going to give him a cavity. He took his black with a little cream. "Five?"

"Is that too many?"

Steeling himself, he said, "Nope, that's great. Thank you, honey." At least she'd walked away as he took a sip, so she didn't see him cringing in horror.

It was a windy morning, the snow coming down in thick clumps. Bundled, Eve walked with purpose to the box office window at The Palace. "Hi," she said in a perky voice. "I'm Eve Morgan from Crestlane Financial. I have an appointment with Patrick."

"Oh, this way," the woman said, pointing her to the door on her left.

"Thank you!" Eve was buzzed in and strode through, shaking the snow off her.

"Eve Morgan," Patrick said with a big smile as he came up to her. He looked the same as ever, in a slim-fitting suit with a tight haircut and black-framed glasses.

She beamed. "Patrick."

They shook hands. "How long has it been?" he asked.

"About…" She tilted her head. "Two years since you left me for Apex East." The words were delivered in a teasing manner, though. She had no hard feelings—not anymore.

He groaned and stuck his hands into his pants pockets. "Don't remind me. I'm down ten percent."

"That serves you right!" she said, and they laughed.

"You here to steal me back?" he asked and led her into the theater.

"No, actually, I'm here to ask for a favor." Eve swept her hair away from her forehead to disguise the slight tremble in her hands. When was the last time she'd felt nerves while trying to close a deal? She couldn't recall. But they'd never had the stakes that this did. They'd been about money, not matters of the heart.

"Concert tickets?" he offered.

"That would be great."

"Who do you want to see?"

Here we go. "I want to see Max Wingford on Christmas Eve."

He eyed her in confusion. No doubt Patrick knew all the big stars around; The Palace was a draw for many artists, upcoming and established. "Who?"

"He is amazing," she said, warming into her pitch, "and he had an audition with you the other night that he missed because of me."

He gave a knowing look. "One of your clients, right?"

"No, actually, he and his sister won *America's Got Music* a few years back," she explained.

That sparked recognition in his eyes. It was a popular show. "I remember. They were good. Whatever happened to them?"

"She died in a car accident."

"How awful."

"I know. It's terrible." She nodded in agreement. "He doesn't even know I'm here." Drawing in a deep breath, she said, "I just think that if you saw him, you would see how great he is." With every cell in her body, she hoped he would agree to give Max a chance.

He didn't seem convinced, though. "We have a pretty full lineup," he hedged.

"Of course," she said with a smile. "Just hear him. That's all I ask." If she could keep this as low-pressure as possible, she had a better chance of getting him to agree. And once he actually heard Max perform, he'd see what a talent the man was.

But she had to get him here.

Patrick eyed her, clearly curious. Eve had never been one to ask personal favors of people, especially not clients, so she imagined he realized this was a big deal. "It's that important to you?"

"It really is."

With a nod, he dug into his jacket's inner pocket. "Here's my card," he said, handing it to her. All the tension in her body seeped away. *Yes!* "Have him call me."

Eve was so giddy she could scream. "Thanks so much!" she cried out, wrapping the surprised man in a hug.

"And... ?" he asked her with a knowing wink.

Oh, she knew what he was seeking from her—financial advice, a tip or two. This she could do for him as a thank you. "Well," she said, leaning toward him and speaking in a conspiratorial whisper, "Medi-Den is primed for a run. Now, you call those fools over at Apex East and have them make a buy."

He beamed, and she knew he was seeing dollar signs. Eve was good at her job—or she had been, anyway. The least she could do was share that knowledge with him in appreciation. "Thank you," he said. She was sure that as soon as she left, he'd be running to the phone and making orders.

Apex East would appreciate the tip, too. After all,

she'd poached enough clients from them in the past. Wouldn't hurt to even it out a bit.

They said their goodbyes, and Eve headed toward the door, feeling light as air as she tucked the business card into her pocket. Part one of her plan, done. She was making real progress. And it felt good. Really good.

This wasn't about her, though. The good feelings came from helping Max achieve his dreams. From doing something selfless for another person. And she was glad she'd been able to pull some strings to make that happen.

When she stepped into the chilly air, Pearl was standing there, eyeing her with a brow raised. "You're breaking the rules," she started.

"He won't remember anyway," she interrupted. "Besides, if Patrick doesn't like him, he won't hire him." She knew this was... well, bending the rules, to say the least, but it was effective, and that was what mattered.

"You'd better hope that stock goes up."

"I know. Is there anything we can do to make it happen?" Maybe Pearl had some kind of angel magic that helped her nudge it in the right direction.

"No," Pearl said emphatically.

Oh, blast. Too bad, because that would have been super useful. Well, Eve would just have to hope it would all pan out. As long as Patrick was happy, Max would have his perfect opportunity to audition. The man would blow Patrick away with his talent, and then he'd be back on the music track he'd abandoned after his sister died.

Pearl vanished, leaving Eve to mull things over by herself. She only had today and tomorrow left with Max and Lauren. It was do-or-die time. So to speak, anyway. She bit back a sarcastic laugh. But the pressure was on for this to succeed.

How would Max react? Would he be nervous? Glad she'd helped him get another chance? She felt so guilty that she'd caused him to be late for the audition. The first major step he'd taken in two years, and she'd wrecked it.

At least she was able to make up for it. That was worth something.

With part of her plan underway, she had to ponder how to confront Max about not letting go of Lauren. Because if he did, she knew he'd regret it. Sure, he'd try to see her, but the space would grow until it was too big to breach. It had happened with her and her brother... and he was only a half hour away from her.

And besides, Lauren needed Max. Her mom had known that. Eve needed to help him realize that he was the perfect guardian for the little girl. The thought of Lauren being in Florida, leaving her home behind to start all over, made Eve's heart hurt.

The audition was actually the easy part to finagle. The hard part would be getting Max to listen to reason about why he should stand up and fight to keep Lauren.

Chapter Nine

Pearl left Eve alone, and Eve walked through the streets on her way to Max's place. It would be a bit of a haul to get there, but she had the time. Tomorrow was her last day on earth, so today had to count big time. She wanted to absorb as much as she could.

Christmas shoppers packed the sidewalks, busy popping in and out of stores, laden with bags and packages. Eve had never been one of them, sending her assistant out to do her shopping instead.

Christmas lights sparkled on trees, and the snowfall had lightened enough that it was just mild flurries at this point. Eve gave a bittersweet smile as she saw kids running around, sticking out their tongues to catch errant flakes. Their parents stood nearby and shook their heads with bemused laughter.

She was going to miss all of this, and she'd only just discovered it five days ago. The world had such beautiful things to show her—if only she'd taken the time to pay attention before. Now, she was scrounging the hours to make memories that would have to last for eternity.

Eve turned a corner and saw Carter standing there with his wife and two kids. He grinned at the group and pointed to the presents in their hands. Her stomach lurched, and she immediately ducked away to keep him from seeing her, heading a different direction to avoid being in their paths.

Pearl would be furious for sure if he spotted her.

She walked past a woman with a stand set up to sell scarves and hats. The bold colors caught her eye, and she stalled. "Hi," Eve said to her.

"Oh!" the woman said, offering a wide smile. "Christmas scarves? Keep you warm on a cold night."

"Yes," Eve said. "I'll take… this one, please." She pointed at a festive scarf bearing the image of a reindeer, then paused. "You know what? Make it two."

"All right!" The woman tugged two down.

She paid for the scarves and wrapped one around her neck. Maybe Max would like the other scarf. And after she was gone, there would be some small, tangible proof that she'd been here, in his life, even if he didn't remember it.

Her throat grew tight, and she swallowed. Good thing angels didn't cry, because right now, she wanted to sob.

Eve made it to Max's front door, the soft sound of guitar strumming wafting down the apartment hallway. She lifted her fist to knock, then stopped to listen.

He was playing. Was it an original composition? She remembered seeing his guitars when she'd come over to help decorate the tree. Maybe he'd been inspired enough by the holiday season to write something fresh, or he was healed enough to sing the songs he used to perform with his sister.

Her heart flipped in joy as he sang and played, pleasure ringing through in his voice. She couldn't wait to give him Patrick's business card and tell him he had an audition. Doing this for him no longer felt like a job—it was an act she did because she cared.

She deeply cared.

Eve finally knocked. The guitar stopped. The door opened.

Max blinked in surprise, though he seemed to welcome her unexpected presence. The warmth in his eyes made her shiver all over. "Well, hi."

"Hi." She lifted the scarf she was carrying and wrapped it around his neck.

He smirked. "How did you know I wanted one of these?"

"I know things," she retorted, grinning back.

Max stepped away and opened the door wider to invite her in.

Eve tugged her coat off and looked around. Sure enough, there was his guitar, resting on a chair. And was that sheet music? She spied a pencil nearby. He *was* writing original pieces now. She couldn't help but feel pleased at the sight.

Then she realized the apartment was quiet.

"Where's Lauren?" she asked.

"Her grandparents took her to lunch," he said, tossing a loose end of the scarf over his shoulder with a flourish.

"Well, then," she declared as she reached into her pants pocket, "I'll give these to you." She presented him with a handful of concert tickets for Christmas Eve at The Palace. "For Lauren, her grandparents, Sally, and Joe. And you'll be there, too—but you're not going to be in the audience."

He stared at the tickets, confusion clear in his eyes.

"Because," she continued as she whipped out the business card, "he's waiting for your call."

Max took the card and eyed it. "For…"

"The audition! The one you missed. He used to be a client," she explained.

Max didn't seem as excited as she thought he would be. He frowned. "So you bribed him?"

"No," she hastened to explain. This wasn't going how she'd thought it would. But perhaps he was anxious. After all, it was a big deal, and very important to him. "He knows your sister and you from the show."

There was a long pause as Max stared hard at the card. When he looked up at Eve, his eyes were flat, and her stomach twisted. "I appreciate the gesture," he said, "but that part of my life is over." He handed her the card back and walked away, taking off the scarf.

Eve stared in shock for a moment, scrambling with what to do. She put the card on the table. "But it doesn't have to be."

"Well, it is," he said simply.

She drew in a steadying breath and pressed her hands together. "Okay, look. I don't know a lot about Christmas," she admitted, "but I do know it's about faith."

Max didn't look at her. Instead, he picked up his guitar and moved to another room.

"Have faith in yourself, Max," she pleaded. "I mean, don't give up on your music. Don't give up on anything you love."

That got his attention. He spun around and held up his hands. "I'm sorry, but you have no idea what I'm going through." His eyes, his words, were heated.

True. She didn't. Not his personal experience. But she knew about missed opportunities and how much it hurt to regret them. Max shouldn't go through that kind of pain. "I know that life is short." He walked by her again, and she grabbed his arm to get him to look at her. "I know you can't undo things," she added. Could he hear the truth ringing in her voice?

"You think it's easy for me to give away the things I love most?" he challenged.

"Eve," Lauren said from the doorway, coming in with a smile on her face. She walked to her and Max. Marla and Ben were behind her.

"You guys have fun?" Max asked, his tone strained.

"Lots of fun. Right, sweetie?" Marla said.

"Guess what?" Lauren asked, eyeing them both. "I'm going to live with Grandma and Grandpa in Florida."

Max stiffened, and Eve bit her lower lip, watching the scene play out.

"We didn't say anything," Marla explained in a quiet voice. "She did."

"I've been thinking about it. It's better for you, Uncle Max," Lauren said. The smile was there but not quite in her eyes. She was clearly doing this for Max's benefit, and Eve's heart broke a little at the sight.

The girl was willing to leave so she could try to make him happy, relieve him of the burden of caring for her.

Eve almost couldn't bear it.

"Why would you say that?" he asked softly. His eyes were pained.

No one spoke.

"You have your music again," Lauren answered. The passion of her belief came through loud and clear in her words. This was her gift to Max. "You can stay up late and be a night owl. And you won't be alone anymore because now you have Eve."

Crud. Eve's heart kicked against her ribs. The girl had it wrong, all wrong. "Lauren, that is not—"

"Grandma and Grandpa will take good care of me," she continued to Max. Marla and Ben glanced at each other, conflict clear on their faces. This was what they wanted, yes, but they could tell she was trying to justify it for Max's sake. "They have a pool, and you can come visit." She kept her chin up, kept a brave face as she spoke, and Eve felt herself breaking apart at the love this child had for her uncle. She knew Lauren wanted to be here with him. How could he let her go?

Max didn't speak for a moment. "Lauren," he started.

"It's settled." Lauren stepped away and went to her room, closing the door behind her.

No one said a word, like they were all reeling from what had just happened.

"I'm sorry," Ben offered. "She just came out with it."

Marla seemed to rally, shedding her earlier guilt. "It's for the best, Max. You'll see." She gave him a curt nod.

The grandparents left, and Eve and Max were alone in the living room.

Max's jaw was tight. "I guess that's what she wants," he said and waved his hands in a dismissive manner.

Was he totally blind? Couldn't he see the pain in Lauren's eyes as she'd told him that? "No, she's just doing it because she thinks that's what *you* want," Eve said. She reached over and touched Max's arm, needing to feel connected with him. Everything had gone wrong. Her offer for the audition had turned him off, and now Lauren was going to leave. "She's trying to make it easier on you."

He didn't look at her.

"Go in there, talk to her," Eve urged.

"And say what?" he asked hotly. "Who am I

kidding? I'm not a parent." Defeat was written all over his face. "She's only nine. I mean, what happens when she's a teenager, slamming doors?"

"You are going to figure it out," she said emphatically and tugged him to sit on the couch beside her. There was still a chance here for her to be the voice of reason. For her to help him see how much Lauren needed him.

Max didn't realize his worth—in music, or in being there for his niece. How could he not see the joy he brought to those around him? And why wouldn't he fight for what was important? It was so frustrating.

She leaned close and squeezed his upper arm. All she wanted to do was help him, comfort him. "Lauren's parents could have chosen anyone. And they chose you." She paused. "You and Lauren belong together."

Max stared straight ahead still. She wasn't getting through to him.

"I made a lot of mistakes in my life," Eve admitted. All she had left was to drop her guard and let him understand why she was so emphatic about this. She couldn't tell him she was an angel, but she could let him see how much he'd regret it if Lauren moved away. "I had so many wonderful things in front of me, but I didn't even see them." She drew in a shaky breath. "Lauren is right in front of you. Don't push her away." Don't be like I was when I was alive—she wanted to add—keeping everyone close to me at arm's length.

"Like you're pushing me away?" he finally said, turning to face her. His eyes were flat as he regarded her face.

"What?" She wasn't doing that, was she? Here she was, opening up to him. For days, she'd been trying to support him, encourage him. What was that if not the opposite of pushing someone away?

"Oh, come on," he scoffed and stood, his back to her. "I mean, you disappear, I know nothing about you... What am I supposed to think?" He spun around, frustration evident on his brow and in the tightness of his mouth.

"Okay." She rose and walked over to him, sucked in a breath, and laid it all on the line. "Look. No matter what happens, I just want you to know that you and Lauren are the best thing that ever happened to me." Her heart was open now, bared before him.

But he shook his head in disgust. "There it is again. You talk like someone who's about to vanish at any moment."

Her face froze. He'd nailed it without even knowing it. Her throat was tight with all the words stuck inside her, explanations she wasn't allowed to give. Eve wanted to answer, but what could she say?

"Right," he said flatly. "You can't fix your own life, but what, you're going to fix mine?"

The comment stung. "Max..."

"You're going to leave anyway. Please, just go." He crossed his arms and faced the window.

Shut out. She was no longer welcome. Eve forced herself to walk over to her coat and scarf, then picked them up with trembling fingers. She purposely didn't look at the Christmas tree, afraid she'd say something else that would make this mess worse.

She'd failed. Utterly. And just as bad as failing her job, she'd gotten her heart broken along the way. What a wretched mess, too flubbed up for her to salvage the situation. Shame filled her at how she'd screwed up so badly. Maybe Pearl could give her advice.

Except that her deadline was tomorrow. What could she fix in such a short period of time? Max didn't want to see her, and Lauren was going to leave because he wouldn't fight for her.

Eve closed the door quietly behind her and walked away.

Max listened to the sound of the door clicking and sighed. He stared out the window at the snow falling. Tomorrow was Christmas Eve, and things had sure turned sour. How did everything get so messed up?

Part of him wanted to blame Eve for sweeping into their lives and stirring things up. He'd been getting by just fine before her, and then she came and pushed and confused *everything*. This mysterious woman who shared so few glimpses of herself, who talked in riddles, who confused and scared him. Because despite his frustration with her, he was attracted to her.

Deep down, he knew what she was saying was right.

That was the hard part, the part that caused him

the most fear, paralyzed him into panic. Because if he took that business card, went to the audition, and failed, that would be on his own shoulders. Can't fail if you don't try, he thought wryly. It was easier to dwell in the past pain than live in the present and accept the risks that came along with that.

His desire to play music was a risk. She'd called his bluff, though. Forced him to face himself and examine why he was running away.

All the stuff she'd spoken of, the sheer regret in her voice as she'd pleaded with him to not push Lauren away, to not give up on music... What had happened to her, and why wouldn't she open up and tell him?

It was infuriating, even more so because regardless of her personal story, he knew she was telling the truth.

Part of him thought maybe Lauren deserved better than him. Had Becky been nuts to leave her in his care? Or had she thought that *maybe* he'd need Lauren just as much as the girl needed him?

He sat on the couch and mulled over what Eve had said. Was Lauren trying to make it easy on him? Maybe she really wanted to be here, even though it was unorthodox. But even more, maybe she needed to feel like she was wanted.

Oh, he was an idiot. She felt rejected, so she was trying to spare them from the pain of him pushing her away. She was smarter than he'd given her credit for. And he'd broken her heart in the process, forced her to make a call she shouldn't have had to make.

He grabbed his guitar, slinging the strap over his shoulder, moved to her door, then knocked.

"Go away. I've made up my mind," she said.

Max inhaled, then strummed his guitar. "Florida," he sang to the tune of "Jingle Bells," "Florida, Lauren wants to go. But when she flies, she'll realize there"—he thought fast— "isn't any snow." He strummed harder in earnest, sang louder. "Oh, Florida, Florida—everybody!—Lauren wants to go. And when she—"

The door cracked, and he stopped singing, eyeing the girl. Her smile was small, cautious.

"Hi," he murmured.

She opened the door wider to invite him in. He took his guitar off, and they both sat on the end of her bed. Lauren's feet dangled, and she stared at the carpet.

Max sighed. "Look, I really appreciate what you're doing. And if you want to go to your grandparents', I'll visit you all the time. But I really hope you'll stay with me. Because I want you here more than anything in the world."

She looked up at him, a small twinkle of hope in her eyes mingled with a touch of disbelief. "Really?"

"Really." He meant it. Her place was here. He was her family, and she was his, and he couldn't let her go. "I should have told you that." He shook his head in self-deprecation. "I just... I was just scared I couldn't give you all the things that you need."

"But I have everything I need," she said plainly. "I have you."

They looked at each other, understanding between them—openness.

"I'm going make a whole lot of mistakes, you know," he admitted. "And we're going to have some fights. Like, you'll bring a boy over one day, and I'll tell him to get lost…"

At this, Lauren grimaced, sheer disgust on her face. "Boys? Gross."

He held out his fist, and she bumped it.

"That settled?" he asked.

"Settled."

"Come here," he said as he drew her in for a hug.

She squeezed him tight, and for the first time in a long time, he felt like he'd made a good decision—the right decision. "I love you, Uncle Max."

He closed his eyes. "I love you, too, kiddo."

Chapter Ten

E ve sat in her apartment, listless, staring at the blank white wall in front of her. She couldn't seem to muster the desire to move or do anything. Her chest ached with sadness over what had happened earlier that afternoon with Max.

What was she going to do? What *could* she do? She felt helpless, hopeless.

Pearl appeared in front of her, arms crossed, that familiar look on her face—the one that said Eve had a lot of explaining to do.

Eve sighed and looked up, and Pearl's face softened.

"We need to get you out of here," Pearl declared. "Grab your coat."

Part of Eve wanted to ask what the point was, but she knew Pearl was as stubborn as a mule and wouldn't take no for an answer. So she dragged herself off the couch, toward the kitchen counter where she'd tossed her coat earlier.

Once she'd donned it, Pearl grabbed her hand, and they vanished, then reappeared in their old familiar meeting place. The bench was empty, as usual, and the Chicago city skyline glimmered with golden lights.

They settled onto their seats.

"Out with it," Pearl said. "What happened?"

Eve huffed, her breath puffing in front of her, then spilled the beans about everything. "And now I've made it worse. Lauren is leaving because of me."

"No, she's forcing Max to fight for her," Pearl exclaimed. She sounded so sure. But…

"What if he doesn't?" Eve whispered.

"Then we will have accomplished nothing." The words sounded so final, so depressing.

Eve sighed.

"Except for you falling in love," Pearl added.

Eve's heart practically galloped out of her chest. "Who says I'm in love?" Some part of her was desperate to hide her crush from the angel. It couldn't be full-on love, could it? She'd been warned time and again not to get attached, and she'd failed at that too—majorly.

Pearl gave a small smile. "It's so obvious. You think about him all the time. When his heart hurts, your heart hurts. You think more about what he wants than what you want. It's clear." She faced forward and nodded. "That's love."

Okay. Everything she said made sense and was spot-on. Eve had fallen in love with a man she could never have. "Great," she muttered. "So now I get to spend an eternity watching other women bring him casseroles."

"You get used to it." Pearl, always so pragmatic. But Eve didn't think she would. Not when the thought hurt her this deeply.

Was her future sitting right beside her? Angling to take assignments in Chicago so she could steal glimpses of Max from time to time over the years? It sounded sad. "Oh, dear," she said on a low sigh.

"Look. Shake that off for now. There's still time," Pearl said. "And until the last second runs out, there's hope yet that things will work out. Chin up. Stop giving in to your defeatist feelings. You're not a quitter. That's why I knew you'd be perfect for the job."

Eve realized she was trying to rally her spirits, and she appreciated it. "I thought there was a shortage of help," she said, a brow raised.

Pearl shrugged. "Maybe it wasn't as bad as I led you to believe."

A small smile quirked on her lips. "Careful, Pearl. I might start to think you like me."

The angel rolled her eyes. "Let's not get ahead of ourselves here. I'm still your boss, you know." But there was a laugh in her tone that eased some of the hurt in Eve's heart.

"Like I could forget," Eve teased. But she did feel a bit better. Pearl was right—wallowing in sadness wasn't going to help anything.

It was out of her hands now. She'd done everything she could, given it her best shot. All she could hope was that Max would open his eyes and see the wonders in his life before it was too late.

Max stood in front of The Palace for a long moment, staring at the building. His guitar was strapped to his back, and Lauren stood by his side.

His stomach was a tight knot of tension. He couldn't believe he was here. His brain screamed at him to leave, that he wasn't ready. He wasn't talented enough. His songs were uninteresting, uninspired.

Becky would tell him to shut up and go in.

"You can do this," Lauren said with certainty. There was no doubt in her voice, no hesitation. She believed in him.

He wanted to be worthy of such faith. And in order to do that, he had to be strong. Had to take risks. Not just for him, but for her. Because what good was life if you weren't really living? If you weren't striving for the full experience?

Eve had taught him that.

He pushed thoughts of her out of his mind for now, pushed away the intense longing he had to see her face again, hear her sparkling laugh. One problem at a time. He'd deal with that situation later.

For now, he had an appointment to keep.

"Last time I did an audition," he murmured to his niece, "I was with your mom." His heart panged yet again with the loss of her talent, her support.

"But now you have me," Lauren replied.

They looked at each other, and that sadness faded away. "Well, I guess I'm a pretty lucky guy," he said with a smile, and she gave him one back. He reached out to take her hand. "Come on. Let's go."

With purposeful steps, they walked up to the doors and went inside.

Lauren darted through the diner door a moment before Max did, a broad smile splitting her face. She stood on the booth seat beside Ben and declared in a loud voice to everyone in the restaurant, "Hark, ye shepherds, Uncle Max is singing at The Palace on Christmas Eve!"

The entire place erupted in applause and cheers. He gave them all an awkward smile and a hand wave. "Thank you," he said with a slight bow. Leave it to Lauren to make a big production out of it. He loved that kiddo.

When he'd come out of the room, she'd been so nervous, fidgeting in her seat in the waiting area. He'd run over to her and tugged her into his arms, not needing to say a word. She'd squealed and squeezed him tight, whispering that she was proud of him.

It was one of the best moments of his life.

"Way to go, boss," Sally said, offering her fist for a knuckle bump.

"The Palace?" Marla said, admiration clear in her eyes. "Congratulations!"

"Thank you," he told her as he neared their booth. "You're both invited."

"We wouldn't miss it," Ben said.

"Look," Max said as he slid in beside Ben. He rested his forearms on the table and stared straight at Marla, whose smile fell from her face as she saw his mood turn serious. "I hope you're not going to fight me on this, but I can't give her up. And I won't."

Marla frowned in silence.

"I know this situation isn't perfect," he continued, "but she's happy here." That much was evident and had been. He just wished it hadn't taken him so long to realize it.

"Well, because she doesn't know any different," Marla protested.

"She knows what she wants, Marla. And so do I. She belongs here with me. We're a team."

Ben, who'd remained silent until now, piped up. "I agree."

Marla gasped and eyed him. "Ben!"

"You can see how much she adores him," he countered. He turned his attention back to Max. "We'll just have to visit more often. Won't we, Marla?"

The two men looked at the woman in question. She peered out the window, then down at the countertop, brow knitted. She sighed, and the mood shifted at the table. "Well," she said lightly, "maybe the two of you can visit us in Florida."

Max narrowed his eyes. "Hmm. How big is that pool, anyway?"

They all chuckled.

Max released a breath, and with it, the tension he'd been carrying for weeks vanished. Lauren was staying with him. He had a concert—his first one—and Patrick had loved the song he'd auditioned with, declaring it was a winner. Everything was coming together so fantastically.

Well, almost everything. Eve's teasing smile lingered on the edge of his brain. Then her sad eyes when he'd told her to leave.

Like she was a mind reader, Lauren rushed over and hugged Max around the neck. "We've gotta tell Eve," she said with a broad grin.

"Were you listening?" he asked her and wrapped his arms around her, holding her tight. But she was right. "Yeah, we've gotta tell Eve," he echoed. He'd been harsh and cruel, lashing out because of his own fears, his own insecurities. She hadn't deserved that.

His chest burned at the thought of how hurt she'd been.

Max slid out of the booth, Lauren taking his place. He stepped to an empty spot in the diner and grabbed his phone. He owed her an apology. An explanation. He had to hope she'd give him the chance to talk. Maybe he could lure her to the diner with promises of dessert and coffee.

He just needed to see her once more.

Before he could talk himself out of it, he rang her number, his heart in this throat.

It picked up. "Max?"

She didn't sound upset, but it was hard to tell from one word. The tension in him eased a bit. "Eve?"

The phone disconnected, and he got a busy signal, then a recording. *"The number you have reached is temporarily out of service."*

"She's not answering?" Sally asked.

He sighed and hung up the phone. "Out of service."

Sally poured coffee refills for Ben and Marla. "Go see her then."

Good idea. Except... "I don't even know where she lives." He rubbed his brow, exhaling. "I blew it, Sally." Why had he reacted so badly yesterday? She'd asked him to trust her, but he couldn't. And now it was too late.

"Um," Sally said, a lilt in her voice, "maybe not. Max?"

He turned to face Sally and saw her pointing out the window.

Eve. There, in the flesh, a tentative smile on her face.

He couldn't help it. He darted out the door, not even bothering to put on his coat. Snow speckled him lightly, dusting her too. She looked even more beautiful than he remembered.

"Hey," he said. "I've been calling."

She held up her phone, a rueful smile on her face. "I ran out of minutes."

With a groan, Max shook his head. "Ugh, I should have gotten the 180 plan." He stared into her eyes, drinking her in, memorizing every detail. "Look, I don't know what you're going through, but I'm here, and I wanna go through it with you." The words were spilling out of him almost faster than his mouth could keep up. But she was here, and he wasn't going to miss another chance to tell her how he was feeling. "I just, I don't want us to…" He glanced at her phone. "Run out of minutes."

Eve sucked in a shaky breath, her eyes wide. "Max—"

"And I know it sounds crazy, and this is fast, but I…" *Say it.* "I think we belong together."

"You do?" And there, in those rich brown eyes of hers, was a flash of hope. Of something deeper, more resonant. She felt this, too, and every ounce of worry that had been left in him, worry that he'd blown it with her, melted away. "Me too," she said shyly.

They stared at each other for a moment and then they came together, their mouths touching as emotions swirled between them, around them, thicker than the snowfall. He wrapped her tightly in his arms, cupped the back of her head, and embraced this woman who'd brought him back to life.

"Oh," Max said as he pulled back suddenly. "I forgot to tell you the good news. Lauren is staying with me."

Eve's eyes grew huge, and she gasped. "I'm so happy!" she said, bouncing.

"Yeah, and thanks to you, I'm playing The Palace tomorrow night."

That bombshell was met with a moment of stunned silence. "What?" she cried out.

"Yeah, I went—"

"Hey, Max," Sally said from inside the doorway. "There's a Patrick on the phone?"

"Oh, that's the guy!" Max said to Eve. "Don't move," he warned her. He'd run inside quickly to take the call, then come back out here and tell Eve that he wanted to spend Christmas with her. That he wanted to spend a lot of days with her, in fact.

"Okay," she said with a grin.

Max flew to the diner phone and picked it up.

"Max, I called your cell but didn't hear from you," Patrick said in a cheery voice. "I left a message confirming your stage time tomorrow. Be here early so makeup can get you in. We're ready for you to make your big debut."

"Yeah, I got the message. I'm really excited, thank you," he said.

"I'm excited, too. Been a while since we've introduced a new act. I think it's going to be a hit."

Max hoped so too. "Well, I'm going to need a bunch of tickets."

"I think I can scrounge up a few more for you," Patrick said with a laugh. "Don't be late, or I'll be chasing you down."

He laughed. Like that was going to be necessary. He was probably going to be there hours early, just in case. "Thank you. Okay, then. See you tomorrow." He hung up, spun around, and dashed through the diner door.

She wasn't there.

Max glanced up and down the street in confusion. "Eve?" He turned the corner of the diner to see if she was waiting on the other side. "Eve?"

Nothing.

The woman had simply vanished.

Chapter Eleven

Eve's disorientation faded, and she blinked, then stared in shock at the scene around her. She wasn't standing in front of the diner anymore. Instead, she was back on the shores of the beach she and Pearl had visited a week ago—in her all-white getup. The sky was overcast, and the air was decidedly cooler. The scent of water wafted through the breeze. But it was no comfort to Eve.

Pearl strolled beside her, seemingly unfazed by Eve's growing horror. She'd been taken from Max. From Chicago. From Earth.

"Pearl, what am I doing here?" she demanded.

"I knew I was right about you," Pearl said, self-satisfaction evident in her tone. "Your assignment is now over," she tossed out casually, like she wasn't wrecking Eve's world with that declaration.

"But... it isn't Christmas yet. I have time." She needed to go back.

"No, you don't," Pearl said, waving a finger. "Not really."

Eve's whole body ached with sadness, and her throat was tight, her heart squeezing in pain. "But why would you punish me for finishing early? I just started—it can't be over." Her eyes burned, and hot tears slid out.

"I'm not punishing you," Pearl said with a chuckle.

Wait. "Why am I crying?" Eve asked. The tears flowed down her cheeks. "I'm not supposed to be able to cry, right?"

"Because you're not an angel anymore."

Eve stopped at that bombshell of an announcement. "What?"

Pearl sighed and kept walking, forcing Eve to keep up with her. "All right," she said. "I tampered with the rules. Let me tell you." She stopped moving for a moment. "Your body did not die when you fell on the ice."

For a moment, Eve couldn't speak. "You mean I'm actually *alive*?"

"Your body is in the hospital in a coma," Pearl explained. "And I was thinking that if I could help you change your life down there by putting you to work up here, that, uh…" She had the grace to look chagrined. "It would be like a double Christmas miracle, as it were."

"So…" Eve wrapped her head around what Pearl was saying, the full extent of what was going on. "I can go back and," her throat clogged with more tears, "see my family." Her next words broke on a sob of relief. "I can see Max and Lauren!"

"Max and Lauren won't remember you," Pearl said firmly. "They won't remember anything."

Eve took a moment to absorb that. She could have her family, but not her love. A bittersweet miracle, it seemed.

"Now, the light that you shone on them, yes. They'll always have that with them. But they won't remember anything else."

The water lapped the shore in steady waves, and the sand made a hushed sound as they continued walking. Eve was reeling with what she'd just learned. Maybe this didn't have to be a bad thing. If she was on earth, back home, there was hope.

"But I can find them again," she declared. "I can start again." It wouldn't be perfect, of course... Max and Lauren would think she was a stranger. But she could let them get to know her—as a human, one who didn't have a bunch of secrets to hide.

Pearl shook her head. "No, you won't remember any of this. You won't even remember the taxi cab ride." She paused, sighed, and looked at Eve with genuine sadness in her eyes, in her voice. "You won't remember me. You won't remember what it's like to be an angel."

The angel cared for her after all. She had a tough exterior, but deep down, she had a big heart. She believed in Eve and had given her a second chance at life.

Still, Eve was terribly crushed about losing the

memories she had made with Max and Lauren. She'd grown so attached to them. And those kisses she'd shared with Max... they'd lit a fire in her heart she'd never expected.

She loved him, and she'd forget all about it.

"Come," Pearl said, and they vanished.

When they reappeared, it was nighttime in front of the nearly empty diner. Eve's last time of seeing the place—at least, that she would remember. She stared through the window, flashes of memories battering through her mind. Dancing with Max, their connection undeniable as they'd moved slow and close. Sitting on the stool with Lauren at the counter, helping the girl to memorize her lines.

Her very soul hurt with the knowledge that she was losing it all.

"You saved them, Eve," Pearl said in a whisper.

"They saved me," she replied.

Eve stood there, watching the scene unfold before her. Sally brought a cup of coffee over and sat down at a booth, a broad smile on her face as she watched Lauren play with a yo-yo. Max was there, encouraging her with that affection and warmth she'd grown so in love with. Joe slipped in the back and cheered Lauren on, coaching her yo-yo technique.

Max's unorthodox family, one he'd created. One she wasn't a part of.

Eve glanced over to say something to Pearl then realized she was alone. She looked both ways on the sidewalk. No angel in sight. "Pearl? Pearl! Don't go!"

Her head grew light.

"Pearl, wait!" she yelled.

Memories danced through her mind, running backward, one after another—her standing in front of the diner with Max, her leaving his apartment crushed, them dancing, buying a wreath together, the school play, the cab…

Eve's stomach flipped over itself and she became dizzy, faint. The colors faded. Everything faded. All she saw was deep, dark blackness.

"Pearl," she groaned, "wait."

She blinked her eyes open, slowly, gingerly—the overhead light was harsh on her head, which had a slight ache. She was in a hospital, it seemed, from the soft machine beeps near her and the sterile, neutral-toned room she rested in. How did she get here? What happened? She couldn't remember a thing.

Her mind was so fuzzy. There was something important she was dreaming about, something she couldn't quite grasp right now as she woke up. The lingering tendrils of the dream started to fade away.

"I'm here, Miss Morgan," she heard a voice say. She looked down to the foot of the bed. A nurse with a light brown bob and wearing cornflower blue scrubs sat up and came to her side. Her nametag said Pearl. "You're back," she said and clasped Eve's hand.

"I was dreaming," Eve said slowly as she looked around. The colors became brighter, more focused.

She'd hit her head—outside, she thought—when she'd been leaving the office. She remembered that now, kind of. What had happened after that, she had no idea.

"Really?" Pearl said. "What were you dreaming?"

Eve shook off the memory of how she got here and searched her mind for the subject of her dream. She knew it was important, but somehow… it had vanished completely. "I'm not… I'm not sure. I can't remember."

"Never mind, none of that is important," Pearl interjected. "What's important is that you're back, and your family will be so thrilled."

In that moment, there was nothing more that Eve wanted than to see her family. She ached for them in a way she couldn't explain. "Can we call them?"

"Of course," Pearl soothed. "They've been here the whole time." She hitched a thumb toward the door behind her. "I'll get them."

Eve gave the woman a grateful smile.

Pearl opened the door and waved for them to come inside.

Tyler stepped in, wringing his hands. "Eve?" he said. His face was drawn tight with tension. "Thank God. You're back with us." He dropped down and took her hands in his.

There was a compulsion in Eve to make sure Tyler knew how she felt about him. "I need you to know you are an amazing brother, and I'm a terrible, *terrible* sister." She squeezed his hands. "And I'm going start making up for everything that I missed. Right now! You're going to see me at weekends, and dinners, and lunches, and school plays—"

"And now you're scaring me," he said, deadpan.

She laughed lightly and sank back into the bed.

He waved Sherry and the kids in. The boys rushed over, then paused when Sherry warned them to be easy with Eve.

She flung her arms open to hug them, comforting them that it was okay.

Both boys told her they loved her, and she kissed them on the heads, hugging them tightly. Sherry and Tyler talked about how good Eve looked, but she didn't listen closely, too focused on squeezing the breath out of her nephews.

"And no more high heels on winter streets, okay?" Tyler said, pointing at Eve in a warning manner.

She gave a solemn nod. "Yeah. No more a lot of things."

It took a couple of days to get her discharged, but she was finally released from the hospital. Tyler had dropped her off at her apartment complex, then made her swear to call him later so he could check on her. She hugged him and promised. Right now, though, she just wanted to go home and relax for a bit. Maybe take a long bath.

She was meeting Tyler, Sherry, and the boys for Christmas Eve, and she couldn't wait to see them again.

Eve opened her apartment door and stepped in. Home, sweet home. She waited for the familiar comfort to come over her, but there was... nothing. She dropped her purse and coat on the kitchen counter, then looked around.

The place felt so sterile to her. Quiet. She frowned. It was too impersonal in here. She needed to decorate. Get more pictures on the walls. Maybe paint them, even. Add some pillows with color.

The thought of stripping it down and redecorating made her feel better. This wasn't the home she wanted to escape to. It was too cold. She needed to cultivate warmth in her life, and this was as good a place as any to start.

A knock on the door drew her out of her thoughts. She opened it and saw Ruth standing there, Forbes in the woman's arms.

"Hi!" Eve said, smiling. "How are you?"

"He missed you so much," Ruth said as she handed the cat over.

Both women scratched the cat's head. "Oh, I missed you," Eve cooed to Forbes.

"He barely ate without you."

As she eyed Ruth, she felt her heart swell with gratitude. "Ruth, thank you. I am so lucky to have you as a neighbor." Had she ever told the woman that before?

Ruth blinked in disbelief. "You are?"

"Yes, I am," she declared. "Aren't we, Forbes?" She straightened. "You know, I decided I want to redecorate my apartment. Do you... think you might help me a bit? I'm afraid all my color schemes are dark and dreary," she said with a laugh. "And you're so good at it. Your place is bright and inviting."

Ruth flushed with pleasure. "I'd be happy to. I enjoy that kind of thing."

Eve put the cat down and hugged Ruth. "Thank you." The woman eyed her. Eve knew exactly what she was thinking. She chuckled. "Yes, I guess that hit on the head did change me."

"Well, I wasn't going to say it," Ruth drawled, "but..."

They both laughed.

"And, um, if the invitation is still open to come to your place on New Year's Day, I'd love to stop by. Just let me know what I can bring." Eve paused. "Not that I can cook anything, but I'll be happy to buy something."

Ruth gave a broad smile. "Of course, you're invited. And feel free to bring a friend."

Eve's heart squeezed in embarrassment. If only she had friends to invite. Well, maybe Ruth could be one for her, and she'd start making more. "Thanks," she murmured.

Ruth left the apartment with a warm Merry Christmas wish.

Eve grabbed a bottle of water from the fridge. Nothing felt the same anymore. All she knew was that things needed to change. *Something* was different in her heart, maybe due to the hit on her head. She didn't know what the cause was, and she guessed it didn't matter. Eve wasn't satisfied with what she was seeing of her life. She wanted more.

And now was the perfect time to start.

Eve strolled down the sidewalk carrying two cups of coffee. It was a glorious Christmas Eve day. Everyone around her seemed in the best spirits. The air smelled rich with the holiday scents. She felt like this was her first time walking through Chicago during Christmas. When had it gotten so beautiful?

The trees gleaming with lights, the garland wrapped with red velvet ribbons, the festive music... It was enchanting.

She was so glad she was out of the hospital and able to enjoy it.

As Eve approached the Santa ringing his bell, she said, "Hello. I have two coffees—would you like one?" The poor man had to be cold out here.

"Oh!" he said, eyes wide with surprise. "Thanks, miss."

"You're welcome." She dug into her purse and

grabbed money. "And…" She dropped her donation into the jar. "Merry Christmas."

"Merry Christmas to you, too." He sipped the coffee, and she heard his sigh of happiness as she walked away.

Eve made it to her office and entered the room—just as impersonal as her home. That needed to change, too. This place was boring, had no life. After the holidays, she'd ask Liz to help her redecorate. And she'd put up some pictures of her family to remind her of what was really important.

A rap on the glass door drew her attention, and she spun around. "Patrick, hi." There was her appointment.

"Sorry to call you on a holiday, but I figured you'd be working anyway," he said.

"It was so nice to hear from you," she said. "Come on in!"

"I've been thinking about you recently," he said as they took a seat on the sofas in her office. "How long has it been?"

She tilted her head in thought. "Uh, gosh…" Eve swept the hair away from her brow. "Two years? You left me for Apex East."

He nodded, studying her. "Well, I'm ready to come back if you'll take me."

The offer should have excited her—a deal landing on her lap. This was a dream, right? Except… it didn't feel right. The idea of poaching this man and claiming it as some sort of prize wasn't appealing to her. "Gosh, um… Well, I would never refuse a client, but I'm going to do you one better. I'm going to have Tom Carter give you a call. He is a senior analyst here at the firm, he's been here a lot longer than I have, and he has never had a client leave him—he's *that* good."

Patrick stared at her in silence for a long moment. "You're referring me to a colleague."

She nodded. "Yes."

"You remember the size of my portfolio, right?" he asked with a smirk.

"Yes," she said, laughing, and couldn't resist adding, "though I'm sure it's a little smaller than when you left me."

That got him to chuckle. "Carter, huh?"

"Trust me on this."

"Okay." Patrick nodded and stood, and she followed suit. They shook hands.

"How's business at The Palace?" she asked.

"It's great," he said, enthusiasm clear in his tone. "You should come down and check it out yourself. We're having a new Christmas concert tonight."

It sounded like a lot of fun, except... "Oh gosh, I'm with my family tonight." She couldn't ditch out on Christmas for this.

"Well, bring them. It's a great lineup. I'll leave your names at the door," he offered.

She beamed. "Fantastic! They would love that. Thank you!"

He left, and Liz came down the hall. "Eve!" her assistant said. "We were all so worried!"

"Thanks, Liz," she said and hugged the woman.

"Are you okay?" There was genuine concern in her voice.

"You know what? I feel great." It was true. When was the last time Eve had felt this fantastic? Not just physically, but emotionally, mentally. She'd just given a good referral to Carter, who worked hard and deserved the chance. She was spending time with her family tonight. Life was good.

"What are you doing here?" Liz asked.

"What are *you* doing here?" Eve countered.

"I've been making cold calls for you," she announced, pride in her voice. "And I've got two more potentials. If you can just land one, I'll be the assistant to the firm's newest partner."

"You know," Eve started, "that's amazing. But I have been thinking about this partner thing. What's the rush?"

"You really did hit your head," Liz breathed.

"Yes, and I think it's a good thing," she replied lightly.

"I don't understand." Liz's brows were furrowed.

Eve eyed her. "I want you to forget about the potential client list. I want you to forget about everything I've ever taught you." This woman was slowly becoming like Eve—the old Eve, anyway. And she couldn't bear to see that happen. Someone else letting work become her everything. "The only thing we're going to poach from now on is eggs."

"You're cooking, too, now?" Poor Liz, she looked so confused.

Eve laughed. "Listen, it's Christmas Eve. Let's get out of here."

"Okay." The woman still seemed baffled, but she agreed.

"Let's go shop."

That got Liz's attention, and she perked right up.

They exited the building and stepped outside, Liz sliding her black coat on.

"Where to first?" Eve asked Liz. "I want to get presents for my nephews that aren't lame. And for Tyler and Sherry. I have no idea where to start." It made her a little sad, how she didn't know that much about them anymore. But she was fixing that now.

Liz pursed her lips, deep in thought. "What kinds of things do they like?"

Eve scoured her mind, pulling back memories from a while ago. "I seem to remember Tyler was into the outdoors." She snapped her fingers. "They used to go camping."

Liz beamed. "There's a sporting goods store not far from here. We can flag down a cab and find all kinds of supplies there."

"Perfect." Eve nodded. "Let's get to it." As they settled into the cab they'd fetched, Eve called her brother to let him know about the offered concert tickets. He sounded excited and enthusiastic.

It was going to be a wonderful Christmas Eve. She just knew it.

Chapter Twelve

E ve ushered her family up to the box office booth. A stiff breeze whipped through, and she shivered and laughed with the boys, who tucked themselves deeper into their coats. "All right. Are we ready?" she asked them. "Exciting!" She told the attendant her name and received their tickets.

They found their seats and settled in. Eve stripped out of her coat and reindeer scarf. She couldn't remember where she'd gotten the scarf—maybe from the boys?—but for some reason, she'd wanted to wear it tonight. She looked down the row at Bobby and Caleb, who were laughing quietly among themselves, then down to Tyler, who had his arm around Sherry and was pressing a kiss to her head.

Eve was so glad to be here tonight with them. And yet, something in that tender gesture made a part of her heart chip away. She wanted that for herself—to have someone special to spend the holidays with, to spend *every day* with.

All the work she'd been doing, the endless hours spent in the office, had kept her away from the people she loved and from meeting new people.

Maybe it was time for her to start getting herself out there. Not that she knew how. She was sorely out of practice with dating, much less a relationship.

The crowd murmured, and she found their enthusiasm catching. She clasped her hands in her lap and turned her attention to the stage as the overhead lights dimmed. Eager applause broke out around her.

Patrick came out on stage, and lights flooded him. Musicians sat patiently behind him, ready to perform.

"Happy holidays!" he said with cheer. "And welcome to our tenth annual Christmas Eve concert. Now help me give a big round of applause to our first act of the evening, King of Hearts!"

Applause thundered in the theater, and the band began to play a catchy Christmas tune that had people clapping and swaying along. Eve couldn't stop smiling. How had she hated Christmas music before? What a Scrooge she used to be.

"You're up," Patrick said to Max, who was tuning his guitar behind the curtain. The audience's applause died down as the band before him, a quartet, left the stage. "You ready?"

"I don't even know how I got here," Max admitted. His heart was lodged in his throat, and he was pretty sure he was going to puke.

"Well, you're here, so let's do this thing," Patrick told him.

Rally time.

Becky would want him to get out there and give it his all. And in the audience, he knew Lauren was ready to cheer for him. He wouldn't let her down. Not this time.

Max took a moment to draw in a breath and steady his nerves. It was a good song—a *great* song—and while he had no clue where the inspiration had come from, he was glad it had hit him. He was going to play his heart out.

Patrick slipped onto the stage and went to the microphone. "He won *America's Got Music* years ago, and he's here to perform for you tonight. Please put your hands together for Max Wingford."

Cheering and applause beckoned him to steel himself and step onto the stage. He slid onto the stool in front of the mic. Thankfully, the spotlight on him was too bright to see the audience. He could focus on the music.

"Hi," he said into the mic. He shifted on the stool and gave an awkward laugh. "It's been a while. Um, this is a new song I wrote. I hope you like it. It's, uh, called, uh… 'Christmas Eve.'" Okay, so speaking wasn't his forte. Whatever. He pushed aside his self-doubts and began to play.

As Max Wingford sang, Eve watched him, rapt. He was incredibly talented, his voice inviting and strong. The guitar complemented the music to perfection. And the lyrics themselves… They reached into her chest and tugged at her heart.

"It always feels special this time of year." Eve found herself murmuring along with him as he sang.

"Do you know him?" Tyler asked her.

"No," she said, shaking her head.

"Then how do you know the words?"

Eve bit her lip. How *did* she know the words? Why was it this song felt so familiar to her, though it was an original and not one she'd ever heard before? "I don't know," she told him.

She was hypnotized as he sang, finding herself humming other lines along with him. She *must have* heard it somewhere. Or maybe it was just that catchy. She couldn't stop looking at his eyes—the intelligence she saw there, the way he showed his passion for singing and playing.

The man was gifted. And she was drawn to him in a way she hadn't felt—ever.

The song ended. The audience erupted, standing for him, and Eve jumped to her feet and clapped until her hands hurt. He looked so humbled, so pleased, that she found her eyes watering in empathy for him. Why did he move her so?

"Wasn't he great?" her brother asked.

"Yeah!" She knew she wanted to hear more.

Max zipped his guitar into its case. He felt almost lightheaded, delirious, riding that music high he hadn't experienced in years.

He'd forgotten.

It was so good to connect with the audience in such an intimate manner—sharing himself, his words, his song. And they'd loved it—he could tell. Even now, with the theater almost empty, he could still hear a few lingering people buzzing about his act.

"You did it, Uncle Max!" Lauren said, clomping across the stage. "You're amazing!"

He turned to her and took her in a big embrace. "Thanks, kiddo." She believed in him, and he was here, and he'd done it.

He'd followed his dream.

"We did it," he told her.

"*You* did it," she corrected.

"You absolutely killed it," Patrick said, pride in his voice as he thrust his hand out for Max to shake. "Call me."

"I will," Max said with a wondering laugh.

Lauren hugged him and went to chatter with Marla and Ben in the lobby.

Max got his stuff together and entered the darkened theater. Stopping halfway down the row, he turned back to look at the stage. He'd been up there. What would Becky have thought of the performance? She'd probably tease him about his stuttering intro.

He smiled, feeling that usual bittersweet sting that came when he thought of her. But it didn't hurt as much as it used to. He felt she would have been proud of him.

He settled into a seat and stared ahead for a few moments, letting himself absorb everything. Christmas Eve. Lauren was staying with him. He'd been in a concert. Things were on the upswing.

Max stood and went to reach for his scarf that he'd draped over the chair. His hand connected with a smaller one.

"Excuse me," a light, feminine voice said. "I just came back to get my scarf."

His eyes connected with hers, and a strange feeling came over him. Those eyes… They seemed familiar somehow. "Oh, that's mine," he said when he spotted his own a couple of seats away. "That is crazy. We have the same one." He chuckled.

"You know what? You were so great," she gushed.

"Oh, thank you," he said, ducking his head down for a moment to smile. "I, um…" He stalled off and looked at her again. "Do we know each other?"

She scrutinized him. "No, I don't think so."

"Huh." Something about this woman was striking him in a vivid way.

"Uncle Max," Lauren said, running down the aisle and distracting him. The woman laughed as the girl launched herself into his arms.

"This is Lauren, my niece," he told the woman. "This is…"

"Eve," she supplied.

"Like Christmas Eve," Lauren said.

"Yes, exactly." She grinned and nodded.

His niece squinted and looked up at Eve. "Are you an angel?" she asked innocently.

The woman laughed and said no, and Max found himself laughing, too.

"I was thinking the same thing," he admitted.

Well, he'd just embarrassed himself. Time to make his exit. "It was nice to meet you."

Her smile was so inviting. "Nice to meet you, too." She headed back down the aisle, took a few steps, then spun around. Her cheeks were flushed a delicate pink that he found adorable. "Um, you know what? I am having a very last-minute Christmas party tomorrow. Do you guys want to come?"

"Yes," he blurted out a split second before Lauren said her own yes. They both laughed.

"Yay!" she said as she dug into her purse. "Bring all of your friends and family."

Lauren gave a frown of disbelief. "All of them?"

"Yeah, it's Christmas." She withdrew a pen and paper.

"Even Joe and Sally?"

"The more the merrier," Eve said as she wrote. She gave Max the card.

"Can I bring anything? Partridge? Pear tree?" he teased.

She tilted her head and said, "I already have three French hens and two turtledoves."

He couldn't help the smirk that spread across his face. "So, you're good for birds."

"I am." She winked. "See you tomorrow."

After she left, Max gave Lauren a smug smile, flashing the address to the little girl. "Read it and weep," he bragged. They bumped fists.

"I can't believe we're decorating your Christmas tree," Caleb said to Eve.

"I know, me neither," she replied. But better late than never, right?

The apartment looked better than ever. Candles burned in clusters all over the place, sending rich holiday scents throughout the rooms. The warm glow from the Christmas tree filled the space with an ambiance it had never seen. The countertops and tables were covered with expanses of food and drink and festive holiday glasses. And music played in the background, providing the perfect soundtrack to the party.

"How come you're so different?" Bobby asked her.

"I don't know," she admitted, "but I like it."

"We do too," he told her.

She stroked his head and beamed at him. "Good."

"Did you guys thank your Aunt Eve for the bikes?" Tyler asked.

"Yes, only twelve times," she said with a laugh. She told the boys, "You know, as soon as that snow melts, all of us are going to ride our bikes around Lake Michigan." How fun would that be? When was the last time she'd ridden a bike? Well, she'd bought one for herself too, and it was in storage, just waiting for adventures.

The door opened, and Eve said, "Ruth! Thank you for coming!" She hugged the woman.

Ruth wore her bright green holiday sweater, the

one with the Christmas lights. "Thank you for having me. I brought you a little something."

"You shouldn't have," Eve chastised gently. When she opened the bag, she saw a matching green sweater and gasped with a laugh. She thanked the woman for the fun gift. "Enjoy," she told her, waving toward the food and drinks.

"Eve," called a familiar voice. Carter.

"I'm so glad you made it," she said, reaching up to give him a kiss on his cheek.

"We wouldn't miss this." Carter introduced her to his family. Then he pulled Eve aside. "I wanted to thank you for the referral."

"Ah," she said with a smile. "You're welcome."

"You know that puts me over the top," he said quietly.

She clapped him on the shoulder and gave him a genuine smile. Carter deserved the promotion, and he'd be perfect for it. Besides, that position would just be more hours of working. Hours that she didn't want to spend in the office anymore. "Yes, I do, Mr. Partner."

"I don't know what's going on with you," he admitted, "but I like it."

"So, this is a party, and we really shouldn't be talking about business, but…" She drew Carter close. "What do you make of Medi-Den?"

He eyed her, then said, "I think it's due for a spike."

"Me too!" she said. "All right, enjoy." She pointed him into the room.

Eve stood back for a moment and watched the

unusual scene unfolding before her—all the bright colors and delicious scents, the massive Christmas tree, her family, her new friends, people filling her apartment with love and laughter.

Her chest grew tight, and she pressed a hand to her heart. This was what she'd been missing out on. This was right, good.

Something had changed in her, and everyone had noticed. She'd been getting by but not really living. But now, she felt awake, inspired, like every day brought the chance to discover something new.

What a great time of the year for her to awaken from her metaphorical slumber.

Lauren walked up to her, pulling her out of her musing with a bright grin on her face.

"Oh, Lauren, I'm so glad you made it!" she declared.

"This is my grandma and grandpa," the girl said, introducing the two older adults behind her.

"Ben. Hi," the man said.

"Hi, I'm Eve," she responded and shook his hand.

"Marla," the woman said. "Thanks for having us,"

"Merry Christmas!" Eve grinned.

"My uncle's on his way up," Lauren told her. "He's in the lobby, signing an autograph."

"Impressive," she said with a nod. "Well, go have fun," she said, indicating they should enter the party. "Merry Christmas!"

"Hello again," said a deep, rumbling voice behind her.

Eve faced Max. He was even more gorgeous than

she remembered. Those chocolate-brown eyes were locked on hers, and his jaw was firm and defined. He had on a black jacket over a deep purple sweater. It took all her effort not to breathe his cologne in deeply—but he smelled so good.

Something about that scent made her want to draw closer.

Behind him, snow fell softly in a pink-orange sky from the setting sun. It was a beautiful Christmas afternoon, sliding into an even more stunning night.

"Hi," she said shyly.

They stood there in silence, looking at each other. Then he shook his head. "Sorry," he said. "I'm staring at you. You're just so… familiar."

She nodded. The same feeling wouldn't let her go either. "I know." She shrugged with a wry grin. "Maybe it's from a past life or something."

"Do you believe in that?"

"Lately?" She drew in a breath. "I've been believing in a lot of things."

"Um…" He thrust a bag at her. "This is for you."

"You shouldn't have," she told him.

He waved off her protest.

She opened the gift bag and pulled out a wreath. Her heart stopped for a moment. "I had this exact wreath when I was a kid," she told him. How could he possibly have known that?

He shook his head, blinking in disbelief, then eyed the scene of the party behind him. "This is beautiful. Great views."

"Do you wanna see?" she asked him.

His eyes grew warm. "Uh-huh."

She felt a flush of anticipation tingle her skin. It didn't matter why she was so drawn to Max, she supposed. He was here, and she was glad. "Okay."

They walked over to her balcony and took in the skyline.

"Wow," he said, giving a nod of appreciation.

She murmured her agreement. It was impressive.

Max paused, then looked at her. "What are you doing tomorrow?"

Her pulse picked up, an unsteady beat that seemed par for the course around this man. She shrugged in a casual manner. "No plans."

"You wanna get some coffee or something?"

A date. Now her heart gave a hard kick against her ribcage. "Yeah. I'd like to." She was proud of her voice for staying steady, despite the craziness happening in her chest.

Max looked up and laughed. There was a mistletoe perched right above them. "You know, there's an old holiday custom," he started.

"Yeah, I have heard of it," she said with a grin.

He shook his head with a rueful smile. "You don't have to."

"No," she protested. "I think we *do* have to. Right?" She knew she wanted to. He was pulling her ever closer with some invisible string that tethered them together.

"Maybe you're right," he whispered before he leaned in and captured her mouth in a kiss. It was brief at first, just a hint of lips brushing but enough to make her flush. His eyes darkened, and then he stepped toward her and kissed her in earnest.

Eve wrapped her arms around him, stroking the back of his head. Something about this man felt like home to her. It didn't make sense, but maybe it didn't have to. Maybe she could let go of thinking and just... feel.

Eve closed her eyes, the power of Christmas magic sweeping around her in this perfect moment.

Farther down on the balcony, the two kissers were being watched, though they didn't know.

"How did you pull that off?" Becky asked Pearl, shaking her head in disbelief. She'd never seen her brother like this—glowing with an inner light that illuminated his smile.

"Well, sometimes you have to break the rules," Pearl answered in a knowing fashion.

Whatever she'd done worked like a charm. Becky hadn't been a part of it, but she'd been checking on Max and Lauren when she could and had seen their struggles.

Watching them now, her worries faded away. "Lauren looks so happy." Becky's heart was full to bursting at the sight of her beautiful daughter, sneaking peeks and grinning at Max and Eve kissing. It was evident the girl loved her uncle and was thriving under his care. "So does my brother."

"How's that for a heavenly Christmas?" Pearl said with a smile.

After another moment to enjoy a job well done, the two angels vanished into air to let the lovebirds have their time alone.

Epilogue

One year later

"Eve!" Lauren said as she tugged her thick winter hat on her head. "Is it time to go yet? Please?"

Shaking her head, Eve laughed. "The ice skating rink isn't going anywhere," she teased the girl. "And we have to wait on your uncle. He isn't back from whatever errands he's running."

Eve had agreed to watch Lauren while he ran around to get a couple of last-minute Christmas gifts. She'd harassed him about waiting until Christmas Eve to finish his shopping, but he'd taken the ribbing in stride, kissing her on the nose and thanking her.

Lauren slumped on the couch in frustration.

Eve reached over and tickled her. "Don't be a grump," she said in a deep voice. "We have lots of fun things planned today." First, they were going to the rink for skating, meeting her brother and his family there. Then the whole group of them were heading back to Eve's apartment for dinner and dessert.

Max came barreling through the door. "Who's ready to watch me fall on the ice?" he sang. Lauren leaped up and clapped. "It's been a year... since I fell down..." he crooned and paused, letting the girl finish the next line. It had become their game, one they'd taken back up based on something he used to do with his sister.

Lauren tilted her head. "That's why... you shouldn't... clown around," she finished, a triumphant grin on her face.

He bumped her fist. "That was excellent, kiddo. You're talented at this. Maybe you can write my next album."

"We should go," Eve said with a laugh. "Lauren's going to jump out of her skin in anticipation."

Max threaded his fingers through hers, and she felt that familiar leap in her pulse at the contact. "Hi, beautiful," he murmured then brushed his lips against hers.

"Hi," she breathed back. "I missed you."

When he pulled away, his eyes were twinkling. "So, you've never been skating, huh?"

"Well..." she hedged. "Technically, once, when I was eight. Tyler skated circles around me, so I got mad and tried to race him. I ended up eating ice." She shook her head and laughed at the memory. "Even then, I was so stubborn."

Max stroked her face. "I love your stubborn side."

They exited his apartment and headed outside. The air was crisp, the sun shining. Lauren bounded down the sidewalk just ahead of them, skates bouncing by their strings dangling on her shoulder, yammering a mile a minute about how excited she was to skate with Eve's nephews. The three of them had clicked instantly last Christmas when they'd met, and they'd been as thick as thieves ever since.

"Did you get your shopping done?" Eve asked Max. "Wait a minute. Where are your bags?" She eyed him with suspicion. "You didn't bring anything in."

He clucked his tongue. "So nosy," he chided. "Maybe I hid the gifts before I came inside. We do have storage, you know."

Eve rolled her eyes. "Yeah, yeah."

They made it to the rink, and Lauren strapped into her skates. "Watch me, Uncle Max!" she said proudly.

"Those inline skates you got her for her birthday are really paying off," Max murmured as Lauren kept her balance on the ice.

Eve flushed with pleasure. "Well, you mentioned she liked skating. I figured the year-round practice would help." She shook her head. "Now, are you going to rent your skates or just stand here and be a chicken?"

"Me?" he gasped, pretending to be affronted. He glared at her. "I'll have you know, I'm not scared. I'm just smart. Smart people don't fall on the ice, because they know it's a death trap."

"You're also dramatic," she said drolly.

He stepped toward her, and her heart jumped in

her throat at his proximity. "I think you happen to like my drama." Before he kissed her, he pulled back, emotion flickering in his eyes.

"You okay?" she asked.

"I love you," he told her, the words flowing out as easy as a breath.

Eve never got tired of hearing him say that. "I love you too," she replied, stroking his cheek.

"The first time I saw you," he said, "I was drawn to you. Not just your beauty, but your smile. You have this fire in you that inspired me."

Her cheeks burst into flame. Max had told her that the album he was finishing in the recording studio had more than a couple of songs about their relationship. He hadn't let her listen to it yet, but she was eager to do so. "You're sweet," she whispered.

How had she gotten so lucky as to be with this wonderful man?

Ever since she'd hit her head and her life had changed, things had gotten so much better. She spent less time at work, and the payoffs were priceless. She saw her family more, got to know the boys and cheer them on at their practices. She and Lauren had grown close and bonded.

And she and Max... Well, she'd never let someone into her life the way she had with him. They'd shared secrets, confessions, hopes, and dreams.

"I was going to wait until tomorrow," Max said, digging into his pocket. "But I can't." On the sidewalk, he dropped down to one knee and opened his hand.

There was a small box in his palm. He flicked the lid up to reveal a brilliant solitaire diamond.

Eve's breath swept out of her lungs, and she trembled.

"Eve." Max took her shaking fingers in his free hand. "Be my wife. I'll spend the rest of my days thanking you for being by my side, loving you for who you are, and supporting you in all your dreams."

It took her a moment to speak. Her eyes burned with unshed tears. "Yes," she managed to get out.

Max stood, his face etched with relief, and he slid the ring onto her finger.

Applause burst out around them, and Eve laughed a little. Max didn't seem to notice, though. He tugged her in for a kiss that left her breathless, unable to focus on anything but him.

Eve lost track of time. She was too busy wrapped in his arms, the place where she felt safe and loved. This man, who had opened his life to her, had helped her learn how to live and take chances.

When she finally pulled back, drawing in unsteady breaths, they stared at each other, mouths swollen, eyes bright.

"I love you, Eve Morgan," he said quietly.

"I love you, Max Wingford," she replied. The ring wrapped around her finger was a promise. A wish. A dream.

Eve used to dread Christmas. But now it had an extra special meaning in her heart, and she'd hold the holiday dear from this point on. Christmas had brought Max and Lauren to her—and her family, too.

"Let's go tell Lauren," he said with a crooked grin.

They threaded their fingers together. Eve looked up at the man she was madly in love with. "Yes, let's."

Heavenly Angel Food Cake with Vanilla Bean Crème Anglaise

A Hallmark Original Recipe

In *A Heavenly Christmas*, Eve learns that angels can eat as much as they want without gaining weight, so at Max's diner, she orders two kinds of pie and a slice of angel food cake. This recipe makes an angel food cake that's light, fluffy, and well, heavenly.

Yield: 1 cake (16 servings)
Prep Time: 45 minutes
Bake Time: 45 minutes
Total Time: 2½ hours

INGREDIENTS

Angel Food Cake:
- 12 large egg whites, room temperature
- 1 teaspoon vanilla extract
- ½ teaspoon kosher salt
- 1½ teaspoons cream of tartar
- 1½ cups white sugar, divided
- 1 cup cake flour

Crème Anglaise:
- 2 cups heavy cream
- ½ cup sugar
- ½ vanilla bean, split, seeds scraped
- 4 large egg yolks, whisked
- ¼ cup powdered confectioner's sugar
- 3 cups fresh berries (blueberries, strawberries, blackberries, raspberries)
- ½ cup white sugar

DIRECTIONS

1. To prepare angel food cake: preheat oven to 325°F. Combine egg whites, vanilla and salt in a mixing bowl; using a wire whip attachment, beat on medium speed until soft peaks form.

Add cream of tartar; beat on high speed until glossy stiff peaks form.

2. Remove bowl from mixer stand. Using a soft spatula, fold ¾ cup sugar into beaten egg whites, ¼ cup at a time.

3. In a separate bowl, sift cake flour and ¾ cup sugar together; gradually fold into egg mixture. Gently spoon into an ungreased 10-inch tube pan.

4. Bake for 45 minutes, or until cake top springs back when touched. Immediately invert pan; cool for 1½ hours. Loosen edges around the cake with a knife to remove from pan.

5. To prepare crème anglaise: combine heavy cream, sugar, vanilla bean and scraped seeds in a medium saucepan; heat to a simmer. Remove from heat.

6. Slowly whisk 1 cup hot cream mixture into egg yolks, ¼ cup at a time. Gradually add egg yolk mixture into saucepan, whisking constantly. Stir over low heat with a wooden spoon until custard thickens, about 5 minutes. Strain sauce into bowl, cover and chill. (Custard can be made 1 day ahead.)

7. To assemble dessert: sift powdered sugar generously over top and sides of angel food cake. Dredge berries in sugar and arrange over top of cake.

8. To serve: using a serrated knife, slice cake; top each slice of angel food cake and berries with 2 tablespoons crème anglaise.

Thanks so much for reading *A Heavenly Christmas*. We hope you enjoyed it!

You might also like these other books from Hallmark Publishing:

Christmas in Homestead
Journey Back to Christmas
Love You Like Christmas
A Dash of Love
Moonlight in Vermont
Love Locks

For information about our new releases and exclusive offers, sign up for our free newsletter at hallmarkchannel.com/hallmark-publishing-newsletter

You can also connect with us here:

Facebook.com/HallmarkPublishing

Twitter.com/HallmarkPublish

Journey Back to Christmas

Leigh Duncan

Chapter One

December, 1945

*H*er purse meticulously balanced in her lap, Hanna Morse crossed her ankles and pushed down a quiver of anticipation as the heavy curtains pulled away from the movie screen. She aimed a brave smile at the tall brunette sitting beside her, glad she'd let Dottie talk her into coming to the theater tonight. Moping around the house certainly wasn't doing her any good.

It had been six months since that terrible day when the telegram arrived. Six months, and she still couldn't make it through the day—or the night—without tears.

But tonight, she'd let Dottie convince her to take in a picture show. While she'd never get over the pain of losing Chet, she needed to escape her grief just for a little while. To laugh, to enjoy life. At least, long enough to watch a movie.

Lights flickered on the screen. Hanna straightened.

Dottie had promised the movie was a good one—a comedy starring Frank Sinatra and Gene Kelly. It had been so long since she'd laughed out loud that she'd nearly forgotten what her own laughter sounded like. Looking forward to it, she let herself relax.

But instead of the opening credits, the screen filled with images of soldiers marching through New York City. Unprepared, Hanna tensed as the voice of the newscaster filled the theater.

"New York pays tribute to the American foot soldier. These men were chosen to represent all the ten million soldiers of the United States Army. Gliders fly overhead as the city roars its welcome home to the thirteen thousand veterans who fought from Sicily and Italy through Normandy, Holland and Germany. Four million New Yorkers line the four-and-a-half-mile parade route to greet the men…"

She pressed shaky fingers beneath her eyes, straightened her shoulders, and took a breath. She could do this. She could sit here while the boys—everyone else's boys—marched beneath the ticker tape thrown from tall buildings while crowds cheered. She could keep a smile on her face while wives and mothers welcomed husbands and sons home from the war. Chet would expect her to do that much. He'd be the first to remind her that others had sacrificed far more than she had. He'd tell her to think about the Sullivan family and all they'd lost. He'd…

But Chet wasn't here. He wasn't among those who were coming home.

And she wasn't that strong.

Abruptly, she stood. Thankful she and Dottie had chosen seats on the aisle, she grabbed her coat and hat and headed for the lobby. As she rushed up the aisle, plush carpet silenced the sound of the black pumps she'd bought especially for this night, her first night out in half a year. The swinging doors opened into a lobby filled with twinkling Christmas lights and bright red ribbons. The decorations announced the happiness of the season. She blinked, struggling against her tears. She thought she had a pretty good chance of winning the battle over her emotions until a whiff of pine from the boughs that hung over the doors and around the window sills reminded her of Chet. The mask of cheery goodwill she did her best to maintain threatened to collapse completely.

Why, oh why, had she agreed to go out with Dottie tonight? She had no business being here. She needed to go home, to lose herself in memories of better times, of better days. Lately, it was the only way she ever got through the long, lonely nights. Even then, she slept in fits and starts. When she did manage to drift off, she dreamed of Chet dying on a field in a foreign country with no one there to comfort him.

Tears stung her eyes in earnest now. Fighting them, she slipped her arms into her coat. She had to leave.

Dottie caught up to her before she made it halfway across the lobby.

She turned to the woman who'd been the best friend a girl could ever ask for during those first, awful days after she'd received the news. "Oh, Dottie," she said, tugging on her gloves. "I don't want you to miss out because of me. Go back inside and watch the movie. I'll be all right. I just…" She sniffled.

"I wouldn't dream of staying without you." Sympathy glinted in Dottie's dark eyes. She overrode Hanna's protest while she put on her own coat. Together, they hurried toward the exit. "Oh, Hanna, I didn't know there'd be a newsreel." Dottie's breath spiraled into a cloud the instant she stepped from the warmth of the theater onto the sidewalk. Behind her, colorful Christmas lights outlined posters of the coming attractions.

"It's not your fault." Hanna stabbed at her tears with gloved fingers that did little more than smear the dampness onto her cheeks, where they froze faster. "Silly me, I… I just, ah…"

"Here." Always prepared, Dottie handed her an embroidered handkerchief she'd pulled from her purse.

Hanna swallowed a sob. Dottie was so kind. Far kinder than a weak-willed woman like her deserved. What was wrong with her? Why couldn't she be stronger? Why couldn't she bury her sorrow and pain? Chet had willingly fought for their country. He was the one who, like so many others, had given his life protecting their freedom while she'd stayed home to watch and wait and support the war effort by buying bonds and saving tin foil. Yet, here she was, in tears again.

Standing in the cold in front of the theater wasn't going to help her get past this, but a walk might clear her head. Mindful of the beautiful but treacherous ice and snow, she started down the sidewalk toward her car with Dottie—bless her—at her side.

She whispered, "I just miss him."

"Of course you do," Dottie agreed.

"Seeing all those soldiers coming home. It just, ah, it breaks me up." She twisted the handkerchief in her hands.

"Of course it does." Dottie leaned down, her voice growing fainter when two women passed them headed in the opposite direction on the sidewalk. "He's your husband."

"Was," Hanna corrected. She had to remember that Chet was gone. Otherwise, a fresh wave of grief would wash over her whenever she thought of him.

"Oh, Hanna, honey. He's still your husband. Nothing changes that."

If only that were true.

More tears hovered near the surface. Any second now, they'd burst through the protective barriers she'd erected around her heart. She tore her gaze from the rooster tail of slush and snow that trailed the tires of a passing car and cast a pleading glance at the friend who was trying so hard to make her feel better.

"Well, you know what I mean." Dottie struggled to offer the right words. "He's still in your heart. You're always going to be Mrs.—" Hanna's expression must have finally registered. "Oh, I'm just making it worse, now, aren't I?"

A muffled sob escaped. The dam broke, and the hot tears ran in rivulets down her cold cheeks.

"Go on and blow." Offering the same kind of advice she'd give one of their patients, Dottie motioned to the handkerchief. She patted the side of a well-stocked purse. "I've got another one in here."

Though her eyes swam, Hanna smiled. No matter how bad things got, she could always count on Dottie to make her laugh. She'd discovered that the day they'd both begun nursing school. They'd been best friends ever since.

"Oh, look at me blubbering." Hanna struggled to pull herself together. "And when all our boys are over there doing something heroic."

"Aw, have a good cry." Dottie patted her shoulder. "Not all of us are born to change the world."

"Yes, but nothing ever got solved by blubbering on a sidewalk, either." That was it, wasn't it? Now, with Chet gone, what use was she? "I'm lost, Dottie," she admitted. "I used to know who I was. I was Mrs. Chet Morse, wife." She sighed. The yellow telegram hadn't just announced Chet's death. In a way, it had marked the end of her life, too. "I wasn't out to change the world. I just wanted to make a happy home for my husband. And now…" She shook her head.

Now, what?

"I don't have any purpose at all." There, she'd said it. Without Chet, without a husband to make a home for, without children to raise, what was she supposed to do with the rest of her life?

"Well," Dottie tilted her head, "you could walk me to the square."

The suggestion was so surprising that she *tsked*. "That's not exactly a purpose."

"You never know." Dottie smiled slyly. "Even the smallest stone makes a ripple in the water."

Hanna glanced at her friend. She didn't understand what Dottie meant and let her eyebrows bunch. "What stone?"

"It's a saying," Dottie answered with a laugh. "C'mon. They're decorating the gazebo."

Well, she'd wanted to take a walk, she conceded while Dottie threaded their arms together. Maybe her friend was right. A walk past Henderson's Hardware and down Main Street to the gazebo might perk her right up. It couldn't hurt to wander past the Christmas trees the shop owners had erected with such care along the sidewalks. Or to take in all the decorations. Everywhere she looked, greenery tied with bright red ribbons gave windows and storefronts a festive look. The colorful lights against the backdrop of a night sky added such a merry touch that they warmed even her heart. Throughout Central Falls, people were trying so hard to make this a cheerful Christmas homecoming for the soldiers and sailors who'd been away at war.

How could she do any less?

By the time she and Dottie reached the center of town, she'd dried her eyes and banished her tears. She even hummed along when Dottie, hearing the carolers on the square, burst into song. As they approached the gazebo, she squared her shoulders and hid her pain. She refused to dampen the mood of her neighbors who were pitching in to decorate the gathering place at the heart of Central Falls. To prove she'd caught the Christmas spirit, she pulled her camera from her bag and snapped a photo of the women in winter coats and heels who busied themselves untangling strings of lights, while men in suits and hats threaded the strands through hooks attached to the gazebo's eaves. Spotting a former patient, she stopped to say hello.

"How are you doing, Mr. McGregor?" She watched closely, ready to spring into action, as the older gentleman wearing a bowler hat leaned from a tall ladder to place an ornament on the Christmas tree. Mr. McGregor had taken a bad fall last year and broken his collarbone. She knew it still gave him fits. "How's your shoulder these days?"

"Ah, you know. The old rheumatism acts up when there's a storm coming." Carefully, Mr. McGregor worked his way down the rungs of the ladder. Once he had both feet on the floor of the gazebo again, he rubbed his arm. "And I can tell there's a doozy coming in tomorrow."

Hanna nodded. At the hospital this afternoon, she'd overheard sweet old Doc Smithy talking with her favorite patient about a blizzard. "That's what everyone's saying."

Mr. McGregor glanced up as if he could see through the gazebo's pitched roof. "It's a shame, too. Cloud cover is going to hide the comet."

"Oh, darn," Hanna exclaimed with an unexpected pang of disappointment. "I didn't think of that. I was looking forward to seeing it." She shrugged. There were worse things than not seeing a bright light arc across the sky. "But, a big snow storm. It'll be a good night to nestle in, I guess."

Or it would be if she had someone to nestle in with.

She shook the thought aside. Maintaining a brave face, she drew in a steadying breath and issued herself a stern reminder to stay cheerful and upbeat.

But Mr. McGregor only pinned her with a concern that saw through her false bravado. "And how are you holding up?"

Heat flooded her cheeks. Her act wasn't fooling anyone, not if Mr. McGregor's rheumy eyes could see through it. Determined to try harder to do her part, she mustered a smile. "Oh, now, don't you go worrying about me."

"Someone's got to, Nurse Hanna," the old man protested. "You're always taking care of the rest of us."

Genuine warmth deepened her smile. Though she and Chet had talked about moving to the city, people like Mr. McGregor made her glad they'd decided to settle down in Central Falls.

"You'll come to the lighting tomorrow evening, right?" he asked.

The tradition had always been one of the season's highlights. Dressed in their winter finest, practically everyone in town would gather at the square. In the past, she'd enjoyed watching the children, so eager with anticipation that their eyes sparkled while their little feet danced in the snow. There would be caroling and hot chocolate. Some of the younger boys might even have a snowball fight. How could she miss that? Suddenly her plan to spend another evening all alone didn't seem like such a good one. "Oh, I suppose so," she agreed. "I always like seeing the whole town come out for it."

Mr. McGregor studied the gray skies overhead. "Let's just hope the snow holds off."

The words "yes, let's" were on the tip of her tongue. Before she had a chance to say them, though, Dottie rushed over, holding the enormous silver star that would soon grace the top of the gazebo. Holding it up to her face, the brunette struck a silly pose. Hanna had just enough time to snap a picture before they both laughed.

Coming here was a good thing, she decided as she watched her friend act the clown. After all, they said laughter was the best medicine, and Dottie had given them all a healthy dose of it.

Read the rest! *Journey Back to Christmas* is available now.

CPSIA information can be obtained
at www.ICGtesting.com
Printed in the USA
BVHW031517041218
534759BV00001B/22/P

9 781947 892156